THE STORY OF AUSTRALIA

This edition published 2025
by Living Book Press
Copyright © Living Book Press, 2025

ISBN: 978-1-76153-536-9 (hardcover)
         978-1-76153-537-6 (softcover)

First published in 1920.

A catalogue record for this book is available from the National Library of Australia

THE STORY OF AUSTRALIA

by

JOSEPH BRYANT

PREFACE

A BOOK of this modest size could not be a History of Australia; quite evidently much has been omitted. It is, however, an attempt to set up landmarks of history, so that the main road or highway through the years may be intelligently followed, or, in other words, that a clear, general view of the making of Australia as it is to-day may be obtained. Care has been taken to secure historical accuracy on the one hand; while, on the other hand, a story interesting enough for its own sake has been aimed at.

The chapter on "The Bush: its Trees and Flowers" has been read by Mr. R. T. Baker, F.L.S., Curator of the Technological Museum, Sydney; that on "The Bush: its Animals and Birds," by Mr. A. H. S. Lucas, M.A., B.Sc., and that on "Water for Thirsty Lands" by Mr. W. Claude Wilson, C.E. To these gentlemen I am greatly indebted for this service so kindly given.

J. B.

Contents

1.	A HIDDEN COUNTRY AND ITS PEOPLE	1
2.	THE HIDDEN LAND IS FOUND	9
3.	A DUTCH SAILOR	16
4.	THE BRITISH COME TO AUSTRALIA	21
5.	CAPTAIN JAMES COOK	27
6.	BRITISH SETTLEMENT IN AUSTRALIA	34
7.	TROUBLE AND WOOL-GROWING	44
8.	BASS AND FLINDERS	53
9.	EXPANSION AND EXPLORATION	62
10.	OTHER SETTLEMENTS	69
11.	STILL OTHER SETTLEMENTS	79
12.	TWO GREAT EXPLORERS	87
13.	FAILURE AND SUCCESS	97
14.	GOLD	107
15.	FEDERATION	114
16.	WATER FOR THIRSTY LANDS	120
17.	THEN AND NOW	129
18.	THE BUSH: ITS TREES AND FLOWERS	140
19.	THE BUSH: ITS ANIMALS AND BIRDS	150

FOREWORD

By SIR W. P. CULLEN, K.C.M.G.
(*Chief Justice of the Supreme Court of New South Wales;
Chancellor of the University of Sydney*)

THE deep and absorbing love of Australians for their native land was a puzzle to many in the Old World who talked with our soldiers during the Great War, whether during their scanty leisure from service at the front, or when wounds or illness compelled them to quit it for a time or altogether. Well may we love Australia, not only because our very flesh and blood and bone are derived from materials raised from her kindly soil, and our thoughts and feelings and speech have come to us through the people who have made it their home. It is a spacious land, as large as most of the historic countries of Europe put together; a land full of beauty and variety on sea-line and coastland, on the mountains fronting the ocean and the plains stretching back from their far foothills to the centre of the continent. Its people, sprung from a race of pioneers, claim and enjoy free scope for all their energies; for its future they will abate no hope, whatever discouragement may threaten. The choicest and best of their sons spoke for them in deeds, not words, upon the battlefields of Europe, Asia, and Africa when the world's freedom and Australia's called for such as they, telling that pain and death are less evils than failure in a man's duty. Such is the price which Australia's honour and safety called for; and that price mounts up when we add the strenuous labours and privations of her pioneers of former generations, and the long and faithful care wherewith the incomparable fleets of our British nation have guarded us against invasion.

The history of our own country, of the navigators, explorers, and pioneers who served it, must help us to realise what we owe to the men and women who came before us. Our pioneers had half the circumference of the globe stretched between them and their homeland. A wilderness without a rod of cleared land, without a road or house or shop or bank, or church or school or hospital, lay in front of them. If food or clothes ran short a voyage of many months was needed before it could be fetched. Generation after generation of hard work and thrifty self-reliance had to go to the building up of this dear land as we know it now.

Can any one wonder if Australians, when they let themselves think of their country without either foolish boastfulness or equally foolish dispraise, should feel that it lies upon their honour that her good fame shall not suffer at their hands?

CHAPTER I

A HIDDEN COUNTRY AND ITS PEOPLE

FOR a long time in the world's history Australia was a hidden land. Nobody, except the black people who lived in it, knew of its existence. It lay out of sight of the rest of the world, solitary and unnoticed. Daring sea captains made long and perilous voyages searching for unknown lands; but all of them missed Australia. It was not because it was small and hard to find. Australia is twenty-five times the size of the British Isles, and large enough to be ranked as a continent. But its position was remote from civilised lands, and in an out-of-the-way corner of the world as then known. Thus Australia played a game of hide and seek with those old sea rovers.

The inhabitants of this hidden land were sparsely scattered over it, wandering from place to place in small tribes. They were dark brown or black in colour, of about the same average height as the British, and were a very backward people, living in the poorest sort of way. They were without towns, villages, houses, agriculture, pottery, tools—except axes made of sharpened stones—or clothes, except sometimes skins of animals.

The one business in life of these poverty-stricken wandering tribes was to obtain food. Hunting and foraging, varied only by occasional tribal fights, kept them employed. Though Australia provides only scanty natural food supplies, the blacks managed to get a considerable variety of eatables. These included not only kangaroos, opossums and other animals fish and birds; but also ants, grubs, caterpillars, moths, lizards and snakes. White clay even was on their food list, and was looked upon as a great delicacy. Roots and seeds were pounded between two smooth stones, and baked.

They knew just when different articles of food would be in season, and where they could be found. It was the following up of food supplies from one place to another, requiring the moving of their camps, that prevented settlement in villages or towns. At times supplies ran short or failed; and hunger and starvation were experienced. But generally the blacks of Australia lived well in their own rude way, and had their own tasty dishes and titbits.

Some of their methods of securing food were very ingenious. In order to find where wild bees stored their honey, a black would catch a bee, and with a touch of gum stick a tiny bit of white down to its body. He would then let it go and follow the white signal in its flight, noticing where it disappeared into its hive in some hollow tree. Then with his stone axe he would chop into the tree and rob the hive of its honeycomb. The wild bees of Australia have no stings, so he had no difficulty on that score. In order to bag wild ducks a black would bind grass or rushes round his head, and quietly creep or swim up to them, with only his covered head above water. The ducks supposing the green turban to be just a clump of floating weeds would allow him to approach; he would then seize one from beneath and noiselessly wring its neck under water, leaving its body to float while he secured others. With skill and patience and good luck he would get as many as he needed. But not every tribe lived near a haunt of water-fowl and could put roast duck on its bill of fare.

Fire was made by them in the way that is known to all uncivilised peoples. A stick of hard wood, about a foot long, was taken, and its blunt end pressed against a piece of softer wood which was covered with dry leaves or grass. The hard wood stick was then twirled round and round very quickly in the palms of both hands. The pieces became hotter and hotter with the friction and at last sparks were produced and the leaves or grass became alight. Or a piece of wood with a groove cut along it was taken, another piece being rubbed up and down the groove until the sparks appeared. But in moving from place to place the blacks generally took with them a lighted fire stick, which was entrusted to one of the women to carry, thus saving themselves the trouble of going through the process of rubbing the sticks; though an expert black would create the necessary sparks in a very few minutes.

The weapons of the blacks for hunting and fighting were spears made of wood, throwing- sticks, clubs and boomerangs. Except among some tribes in the north of Australia bows and arrows were not known. The boomerang was the most remarkable invention of these people, who had so few ideas of making things. It is a flat piece of hard wood, generally about two feet long and about two inches wide, and bent in the middle. One make of boomerang had this peculiarity—that it could be thrown to a distance, and then, turning back to the spot from which it was thrown, would fall at the thrower's feet. This kind of boomerang was not used for hunting or fighting, but only for display in sport. The other kind of boomerang, used in the chase and for war, was longer and without the side-way twist given in the making of a return boomerang. But war among the Australian blacks was not a very bloodthirsty affair. It usually came about through one tribe trespassing on the hunting grounds of another tribe. When they met in battle each side would make a great noise, shouting threats and taunts, and striking their spears together. Dust was thrown in the air, and a furious scene worked up. When they came to blows they were not often of a deadly character. Presently they had exhausted themselves and tribal honour was satisfied. After the battle the combatants usually feasted together in a great "corroboree," A corroboree is a black's entertainment, consisting of music and dancing, athletic sports, action songs, eating, and some solemn religious rites, all combined in one programme.

Among Australian blacks women were required to do the hard work of the camp, and to carry the loads when camp was moved. The men hunted, and fought, and made weapons; and between times loafed around. The women were drudges and carriers.

A mother would make a portable cradle for her child by putting it into a bag made from the skin of some animal. The bag was hung from her neck and down her back. She could pick up the child by one of its arms and dexterously fling it over her shoulder into this convenient pouch, which left her hands and arms free for other work or other burdens.

Among tribes by rivers or along the sea-coasts, children at a very early age got rough-and-ready lessons in swimming. The mother would swim out holding the child, and then let it go, or would simply throw it into the water. When the child was in danger of drowning she would rescue it. This would be done each day until the child, learning instinctively how to paddle with arms and legs, could keep itself afloat. It soon became expert, and was quickly as much at home in the water as on land.

The marriage laws of these black inhabitants of Australia were most extraordinary. It used to be thought by white people that marriage among them was simply by capture, and that a man just knocked a woman on the head, and carried her off as his wife. This idea was quite a mistake. So far from that being the case, their marriage laws were the most elaborate in the world. These laws were based on a principle called Exogamy, the meaning of which is "marrying out." Each tribe was divided into two or more classes, and these were divided into smaller classes, and these again into yet smaller ones. No one was allowed to marry a member of one of his, or her, own class or sub-classes. He or she must marry out. But not into just any one of the various other classes; oh no! it could only be into a class permitted to him, or her, by these strange marriage laws. The laws as to who and who might marry were a real criss-cross, which white people find very hard to understand. One scientist has said they are "enough to puzzle a Philadelphia lawyer." Yet this backward and ignorant people made the laws, and remembered and handed them down, without any writing, for a great many hundreds of years.

The blacks had their own religious ideas. They believed in good and evil spirits, and in one Great Spirit who was above all. They had no name for that Great Spirit. When they spoke of him, they did it in solemn frightened whispers, as Ngunda; which is not a name, but means simply "He." They believed in magic, and spent their lives in fear of it. Each tribe had its maker of magic, or medicine man. It was thought that he was able to cause sickness, or cure it, as he willed. The way in which he was supposed to cause sickness was by putting evil magic into a stick, or bone, or stone, and then pointing it at the one he wished to sicken. When a man had been pointed at, his only hope was to get the curse taken off by some opposite magic. Very often the man who believed himself to have been pointed at did really sicken and die of very fear. He looked upon himself, and everyone in his tribe looked upon him, as a doomed man. He lost his appetite; no longer went hunting; wondered which day would be his last; had no heart for anything and finally lay down to wait the end: so the end came. The medicine man was believed to be a rain-maker, too, and was very much honoured and feared. Among the religious ideas of the blacks was that of life after death. It was reckoned most unlucky to speak of the dead, and the names of the dead were never mentioned.

In the northern and western parts of Australia numbers of blacks may still be found carrying on their old customs and modes of life. But in the parts now populated by white people they have almost, or altogether, disappeared. They never were at all numerous for such a large country, and were scattered very thinly over it. Since white settlement came they have rapidly become fewer, and it is only in the far back, still unsettled, parts that tribes now exist.

The Governments of the different States make some provision for them; and the Churches have established mission stations, where they can be taught and cared for. But it is quite clear that the Australian blacks are a dying race. This is sad, for in spite of their backwardness, they are in many ways a likeable and teachable people. Black children get on very well at school, and some of them are really clever. The men make good hands on sheep and cattle stations; and the women take up house work quite well. They are a very light-hearted race, full of fun and laughter, are great mimics, and make good musicians.

One of the special attainments of the blacks is that of tracking. They can follow the track of man or animal, where no white man would see the faintest trace. The slightest turn of a twig, or a leaf, or a blade of grass, touched by anything in passing, is guidance enough for their sharp eyes, which see at once the most trivial mark. This art of theirs has often been useful to settlers in the uninhabited forests or plains, and back-country police stations have usually had a black tracker attached to them.

The fatal thing to the blacks is that they cannot settle down permanently, and fit themselves into white man's civilised life. The wandering habit is in their blood. The wild life is the only life for them. As they cannot have that when the country is taken up by white people for farms and sheep and cattle stations, and when towns and villages spring up, the blacks die off more and more. It is sad, but this strange race is vanishing away.

CHAPTER II

THE HIDDEN LAND IS FOUND

WHO was the first to find Australia? No one can tell. There were stories among the ancient Greeks and Romans, and long before their time, about a continent far away in the South. It was thought in olden times that there must be just as much land on one half of the world as on the other, to keep it level. Whether anybody really knew of a great southern land or not, this theory about balancing the world required such a land. It must be there, said these ancients, and so they put it on their maps, guessing at its position and shape. There is a map as far back as the eighth century which shows this southern land, but it is not in the least like Australia.

Then come later maps showing a land which is rather more like the real thing, though very far from correct. These later maps, however, were based upon some very slight knowledge of Australia. Someone had seen its shores and reported about it. "Jave la Grande" it was named. Some of these old maps are highly pictorial. One of them, dated 1546, has on the country intended for Australia pictures of trees and lions and men; and in the surrounding ocean are sea-serpents with a man riding on the back of one of them. Another map is almost covered with drawings quite well done. There is a procession of black men wearing coats, following a man on horseback; and one of the procession holds over the horseman's head a sunshade on a long pole. Houses, camels, horses, and wild-looking men, come into the drawings. These pictures represent the ideas of the map-makers as to what might be in that far-off land. But as time passed on these early maps improved, becoming decidedly more like Australia; and it is evident that some further knowledge of the great South Land had been obtained, though still indefinitely.

It is almost certain that some Portuguese navigator was the first from the outside world to see Australia. But what his name was, or anything else about him, we do not know. Spanish seamen came next. In the year 1605 Pedro Fernandez de Quiros sailed from Callao in South America to find the Great South Land, and take possession of it for the King of Spain. He had already been in those seas with the great Spanish commander Mendana, who had looked for it in vain. De Quiros had three ships. Strange-looking vessels they would seem to us, and very small; though they were reckoned huge affairs in those old days. They rose very high out of the water; their masts and broad sails standing tall above the lofty decks; the ships' sides pierced with openings for the cannons' mouths; the prow of each vessel surmounted by the figure of a saint or angel carved in wood, and richly gilded. Luis Vaez de Torres commanded in the fleet as second to de Quiros.

After many months of sailing, during which several islands were discovered, de Quiros thought he had come to the land he sought. He named it Austrialia (not Australia) del

Espiritu Santo, which means Austrialia of the Holy Ghost. He chose "Austrialia" as a compliment to the King of Spain, who belonged to the Imperial House of Austria. But de Quiros was mistaken as to the land he had reached. It was an island of the New Hebrides group, and not the Great South Land. However, he never found out his mistake. One night he suddenly sailed away with his flag-ship, giving no notice to Torres on his ship near by. It seems most likely that this sudden sailing was not de Quiros' own doing, and that his crew had mutinied and taken charge of the ship. De Quiros arrived after many months at a port in Mexico. When he returned to Spain he begged very hard again and again for ships to visit Austrialia del Espiritu Santo, still believing that it was the Great South Land. At last he determined to undertake the voyage without the aid of the King. But he had waited too long. He died on his way to Lima in South America, from which place he had hoped to sail with his new expedition.

After de Quiros had sailed away so strangely, Torres waited for some time to see whether his commander would return. When he did not come, Torres sailed off on his own account. He very nearly discovered Australia. It is most likely that he did see its coasts in the distance. But if he did, he thought they were only the coasts of another island, such as he had seen many of in those seas. He passed on, and lost his chance of being the discoverer of Australia.

The Dutch followed the Spanish closely in the southern seas. One day in the year 1606 there came sailing towards Australia a Dutch ship named the *Duyfken*, which means

Little Dove. It was a tiny vessel to be on a voyage of discovery in far-off seas but the Dutch were fine sailors, and the skilful captain knew how to navigate his *Little Dove*, with its grey sails for wings, through all weathers and over all seas. This ship had been sent out by the Governor of the Dutch East Indies, whose headquarters were at Batavia, in the island of Java. The captain's instructions were to look for the Great South Land which no one had yet claimed, and which might be a great prize to add to the Dutch possessions. He sailed along the coast of New Guinea already known. Then, without being aware that he had left that island, but believing that its coasts still continued though out of sight, he kept sailing on until he entered a wide opening in the North Coast of Australia. This opening is now known as the Gulf of Carpentaria. The Dutch captain had found Australia; but he did not know that he had found it. He thought it was a continuation of the island of New Guinea.

The name of the staunch little Dutch ship has been known from the first. But the name of her commander was lost, and he could only be spoken of as the "Captain of the *Duyfken*." He was a hero without a name. Quite recently the lost name has been found. Willem Jansz, captain of the *Duyfken* and discoverer unawares of Australia, we salute you!

Jansz sent some of his crew ashore in the Gulf of Carpentaria. They were at once attacked by blacks who had watched the coming of the strange ship, and lay in ambush. Some of the landing party were killed. The country looked very uninviting; provisions were getting short on board; it did not seem worth while to risk the lives of more men; and after sailing some distance into the Gulf, the *Duyfken* was headed round at a point which Jansz named Kaap Keer Weer ("Cape Turn-Again"), and sailed back to Java. The first report given of Australia was a poor one. "A land for the most part desert, and inhabited by cruel, wild, black savages," was the opinion Jansz formed of it.

Ten years after this, another Dutch ship, the *Eendracht*, sailed along the west coast of Australia. Her commander was Dirk Hartog. He landed on a small island, which is now called Dirk Hartog's Island, and set up a post, fastening to it a tin plate with the names of the ship and its officers, and the date of the visit inscribed on it. The little island was left to its wind-swept solitude for eighty years after this. In the year 1697 another Dutch vessel, the *Geelvink* under Captain Vlaming sighted the island. Vlaming landed a party, and Hartog's old post and plate were found. The plate was taken down, and its inscription copied on to a new one put in its place, with something added about Vlaming and the Geelvink. For a hundred years after this the island was unvisited. Then a French ship, the Naturaliste, happened to come along. Hartog's post was found, and Vlaming's tin plate lying at its foot almost buried in sand. It was fixed to the post again. Hartog's original plate, carried away by Vlaming, was found in the Museum at Amsterdam not many years ago.

In the year 1628 a fleet of ten ships sailed from Holland with the intention of possibly making a settlement on the west coast of Australia. A warship, the *Batavia*, under Captain-General Pelsart, went with the fleet as escort. During a storm the *Batavia* became separated from the other ships, and struck a reef about thirty miles off the Australian coast. The reef had been discovered by another Dutch captain some years before, and named by him Houtman's Abrolhos. Pelsart succeeded in landing most of his passengers and crew on some of the small neighbouring islets. There was no fresh water to be found on them, and boats were sent to get supplies from the main-land. Pelsart himself set off with a few men in one of the ship's boats to obtain help from Java. Soon after his departure some of the sailors on one island formed a plot under the leadership of the supercargo, Cornelis by name, to murder the rest of the company, secure all the stores, seize the relief ship when it came, and set out as pirates. They carried out their murderous schemes in part, killing forty or more on the island, and then proceeded to attack those on another. They, however, had been warned, and defended themselves successfully.

Meanwhile Pelsart reached Java, and returned with another ship, the *Saardam*. Cornelis and his band of ruffians in the meantime had decked themselves out in uniforms taken from the wrecked ship. Cornelis himself had been proclaimed Captain-General, and had a body-guard dressed in scarlet. As the *Saardam* drew near, the party on the other island succeeded in giving some warning of trouble. Cornelis and his men, who rowed out to the ship, were foolishly dressed in their finery and carrying arms, which made Pelsart suspicious. When he demanded from them what all this meant, Cornelis replied that he would tell them when he and his men had come on board. At once Pelsart declared that unless they gave up their arms immediately he would sink their boat where it lay. Sullenly the mutineers, who were conducting themselves so stupidly, obeyed. They were then ordered on board, and put in irons.

Pelsart held a council of war, and it did not take long to decide that Cornelis and his fellow scoundrels should be hanged from the yardarms. One hundred and twenty were executed. Two of the mutineers, however, were spared this sentence, and instead were put ashore on the mainland of Australia to take their chance of life or death there. Their chance of life was a poor one, and probably they fell victims to the blacks.

CHAPTER III

A DUTCH SAILOR

A GREAT many Dutch vessels visited the coast of Australia. Some of them did so accidentally, being driven out of their course by storms on their voyages to the Dutch East Indies; and some of them never returned, but met their end in those uncharted seas. In the year 1655 the *Vergulde Draeck* was wrecked on the west coast, and none of her crew were ever heard of again. Seventy-eight thousand silver guilders went down with the ship. Search vessels were sent out, but nothing of ship or crew was found. About the year 1684 the *Ridderscap van Holland* was lost on the same coast. In 1727 the *Zeewyck* was wrecked there; but some of the crew built a raft, and eighty-two persons reached safety, bringing with them two treasure chests.

The best known of all the Dutch captains who sailed in Australian seas is Abel Janszen Tasman. We have interesting accounts of his voyages. On August 14, 1642, he set out from Batavia, with two ships, the *Heemskerck* and the *Zeehaen*. He was directed by the Governor-General, Antonio van Diemen, to make a thorough examination of Australia, and any other lands he might find lying to the south. He sailed first south-west to Mauritius to get the advantage of the trade wind.

Then with this wind filling his sails he sped south-east, and later on full east.

Tasman had a good look-out kept. There was need for it in such unknown seas, where treacherous reefs might be lying in wait anywhere. A man was kept at the masthead night and day, and he would need to sit tight as the vessel rolled and pitched; the long deep swell doing its best to fling him from his perch. A reward was offered to any who discovered land, reefs, or sand-banks. The reward for "keeping their eyes skinned," as sailors say, was three reals and a pot of arrack. A real was a coin worth two pence-halfpenny in English money of that time, and arrack was, of course, something to drink.

After about seven weeks, sailing land was sighted. Tasman named it Van Diemen's Land, after the Governor-General. It bore that name for a long time, but it has been very properly changed to Tasmania, after its discoverer, the brave Dutch captain himself. The weather was very stormy, and Tasman, after touching the west coast, had to stand out to sea again. He returned to a beautiful bay which still bears the name he gave it, Storm Bay. Two boats' crews went ashore, and returned with stories of strange sights and sounds. They saw trees of immense size, with steps five feet apart cut in them. Tasman wrote "Either these people are of prodigious size, or they have some way of climbing trees which we are not used to." The blacks had cut these steps with their stone axes, as they pulled themselves up the tree with their arms and legs round it, using the cuts as resting-places and jumping-points by putting their toes into them. Tasman also reported that a sound like a gong was heard, but he did not know what it was; and there were seen the marks of wild beasts' feet like those of a tiger. He saw smoke rising in several places, but did not come into contact at all with the blacks.

Tasman sailed on again, and after eight days came in sight of a mountainous country, which he named Staaten Land in honour of the States General of Holland, and cast anchor in the strait between what are now known as the North and South Islands of New Zealand. Here he had a fight with the natives, and lost some of his men. Seven canoes full of native warriors surrounded the *Zeehaen*, and five more lay about the *Heemskerck*. They upset a boat's crew from the *Zeehaen*, killing three of them, while the others had a narrow escape, swimming for their lives. Tasman proclaimed the natives as enemies, and naming the spot Massacre Bay he sailed away. He wrote: "Our ship's company would no doubt have taken a severe revenge if the rough weather had not hindered them." He sailed along the west coast of New Zealand, and then swept round into the Pacific Ocean. There he discovered the Friendly Islands (as Captain Cook afterwards named them) and the Fiji Islands, and returned to Batavia after being at sea for ten months.

Tasman was commissioned for a second voyage of discovery in the year 1644, and set sail with three ships, the *Limmen*, the *Zeemeuw*, and the *Braek*. He was told to find out first whether New Guinea was divided from the Great South Land—Australia. Then he was to proceed to Houtman's Abrolhos, and there try to fish up some boxes of six dollars that had gone down with the wreck of the *Batavia* on that dangerous reef. He was also to keep a look-out along the coast where the two mutineers had been landed and left by Captain-General Pelsart; and if he found them he was to give them a passage home. He found neither the lost dollars nor he marooned mutineers, but he did excellent exploring work, and was able to complete a map of the west coast and part of north-west and south coasts of Australia. The trading directions given to Tasman suggested sharp practice. If he found people he could trade with he was to make special inquiries for gold and silver, but he was not to let them see that he cared at all particularly about these precious metals. He was to show them copper, pewter, and lead, and to pretend that they were of more value to him. Then, if the natives could understand, he was to get them to make treaties with Holland. His voyages disappointed the Dutch East India Company in these respects; for Tasman found no lands where gold could be bartered for cheap Dutch goods, or huge fortunes made out of simple, uncivilised races ignorant of their own wealth.

At this time the name New Holland was given to the Great South Land. The Dutch had good right to name it after their own beloved little country far away in Europe; for they had taken much greater interest in it than any other nation, and they might very well have claimed it as a Dutch possession. They did so in a general sort of way, but the only true and rightful claim would have been by making settlements on it. This they did not do, and Australia slipped from them. There are a number of Dutch names on the map of Australia to-day which tell the tale of Dutch seamen or Dutch ships. Cape Leeuwin was so named after the Dutch ship, the *Leeuwin,* which means Lioness. There are Dirk Hartog's Island, Pelsart Group, Duyfken Point, Cape Keer Weer, Geelvink Channel, Arnhem Land, Point Nuyts, and many others, still reminding us of those sturdy sailors with the broad-built ships, which would look so tiny now, and the daring voyages they made to the coasts of Australia.

CHAPTER IV

THE BRITISH COME TO AUSTRALIA

THE first Englishman to come to Australia was William Dampier. He came in bad company. He was one of a party of buccaneers. Their business was to seize Spanish ships, and usually to massacre their crews, and secure their treasure; also to sail into Spanish ports in South America to kill and loot. This sounds very bad: and so it was. But it was regarded at that time as a form of warfare that was allowable. The Spaniards in those days claimed absolute possession of most of the New World, as America was called. They looked upon French or British sailors as trespassers; treating them with great cruelty, imprisoning, hanging, or making slaves of them. The French and British did not spare the Spaniards in return, when they fell into their hands.

For some years Dampier led this life of wild adventure by sea and on land. After being at sea a long time, the vessel he was on board needed to have her sides and keel cleaned, and to be put altogether in repair. A spot where no one was likely to come and surprise them had to be found, and the lonely coast of Australia was chosen. There the vessel, the *Cygnet* by name, was beached. Dampier did not see much of the country, but he formed a very poor opinion of it, and wrote that the blacks were "the miserablest people in the world." After leaving Australia, Dampier became tired of his wild companions, and made his escape from the *Cygnet*. In doing so he took a most perilous voyage in a native canoe to Sumatra, and finally reached England. He published an account in two volumes, of his travels and adventures, entitled *A Voyage Round the World*. The story made Dampier famous, and King William the Third provided him with a ship, the *Roebuck*, carrying a crew of fifty men, twelve guns, and provisions for twenty months, to sail again to the South Seas and make a fuller report about Australia.

The *Roebuck* reached Australia in August 1699, anchoring in a bay, which Dampier called Shark's Bay, because the sailors caught several sharks there, and said that their flesh was very good eating. Dampier then sailed along the coast for about a thousand miles. His first bad impression of Australia was a little improved as he noticed flowers, and trees, and birds which he had not seen on his former visit, but he still thought it the barrenest country on earth. He was much interested in the kangaroo, and was the first to mention this animal, which he called a raccoon, and liked the flavour of as "very good meat."

He tried to get to know some of the blacks, but they would not have anything to do with the pale-faced visitors. On one occasion, he took with him two of his men, and attempted to waylay and capture a black, specially because he wanted to find out where fresh water could be got. The result was a fight, in which one of Dampier's men was nearly killed. In spite of Dampier using his gun the blacks continued to show fight, "tossing up their arms," he wrote, "crying Pooh! Pooh! Pooh!" (very rude of them!) "and coming on afresh with a great noise."

On his return voyage to England, Dampier's ship was wrecked and many papers were lost. But soon he was off again to the South Seas with a small squadron to rob as many Spanish ships as he could catch. The captain of the second ship quarrelled with Dampier and deserted. The mate of this ship, Alexander Selkirk, was reckoned by Dampier to be one of his best sailors, but the mutinous captain wanted to get rid of him and put him ashore on the lonely, uninhabited little island called Juan Fernandez. Four years later Dampier was once more in the South Seas, and calling at the island found Selkirk still alive though "the melancholy and terror of being left alone in such a place," he said, had been almost more than he could bear. Selkirk's experiences gave Daniel Defoe the idea of his famous story, *Robinson Crusoe*.

Dampier's unpleasing and discouraging account of Australia was not likely to lead any one to take much further interest in what was described as such a poor and dreary land; and for seventy years after this Australia was left alone. Dampier was a fine sailor, and could write very fascinating accounts of his voyages; but it is pleasant to think that it was not this buccaneer, but a far nobler and greater man who gave Australia to the British Empire.

There came next into the South Seas one of the greatest of English seamen and explorers, Captain James Cook. He was born at Marton in Cleveland, in Yorkshire, in the year 1728. His father was a farm labourer, and was so poor that he could not afford to send his son to school. Instead of going to school, he went to work on a farm before he was eight years old; his work being to take the horses to drink, to run on errands, and make himself useful in little ways. Mrs. Walker, the wife of the farmer for whom the small boy worked, taught him his letters and some reading. Fortunately for him, a Mr. Skottowe also befriended him, and sent him to school at the age of eight. When he was thirteen he went to learn the business of a village shopkeeper at Staithes, overlooking the North Sea, a few miles from the port of Whitby. James Cook was much more interested in the ships that sailed up and down that busy coast than he was in shopkeeping. His ambition was to be a sailor; to feel the heaving of the waves beneath him, and the rush of the winds around him; and to voyage to far-off lands. Some writers have told of James Cook running away from his shop-keeping, and taking a shilling belonging to his master to help him on his way. Careful inquiry has shown that there is no truth whatever in this. Cook's master saw that he had no liking for his trade, but was bent on going to sea, and persuaded the lad's father to consent to this. So it was that James Cook came one day (a great day it was for him) to Whitby, and was bound apprentice for three years to a firm of ship-owners. The vessel on which he began his seafaring life was a collier, grimy and black with coal dust, and took only short coastal voyages. The apprentice laid himself out to become a capable seaman, and studied nautical books in any spare time he had. He rose to the position of mate, and soon afterwards could have had the command of one of the ships of the firm. But James Cook was not going to be content with commanding a coaling-ship on the North Sea and the Baltic. He gave up the rank he had gained, and entered the Royal Navy as a common sailor. Thus he began at the foot of the ladder on which he was to climb so high. He was sent on board H.M.S. *Eagle*, a fourth-class man-of-war of 60 guns, and a crew of 400, and 56 marines. Before two months were over Cook's ability had been noticed, and he was made Master's Mate.

At that time Great Britain was at war with France, and was determined to take from France her possessions in North America. Cook saw fighting there, and was of special service in charting the St. Lawrence River, up which British ships had to sail against the French. For this service he received a present of £50 from the Government. He studied hard at the science of his profession, and was not going to be content with just a common, every-day knowledge of seafaring. At the age of thirty he was put in command of the schooner *Antelope* for the purpose of making charts of the coast of Newfoundland. While there he took very difficult observations of an eclipse of the sun. His report about it was sent to the Royal Society, which was astonished that any one in Cook's position should be able to take such accurate observations, and send in such a careful and valuable report.

When the war was over, the British Government under-took a scientific expedition to Tahiti, in the South Seas. The object of the expedition was to observe the Transit of Venus, upon which certain astronomical reckonings depended. But the voyage was to become famous for another reason; it was going to lead to the discovery of the east coast of Australia by the British. Cook was chosen to command the ship *Endeavour*, with the scientific party on board. Before he and his ship returned to England he would have claimed the eastern part of Australia as a British possession.

The Dutch had been on the north and west coasts and part of the south coast; but no one had touched the east coast. It remained quite unvisited and unknown. The discovery of it was about to bestow immortal fame upon James Cook, Commander of the good ship *Endeavour*, and give to the British Empire a whole continent.

CHAPTER V

CAPTAIN JAMES COOK

ON August 25, 1768, Cook set sail for Tahiti. His ship, the *Endeavour*, would seem to us ridiculously small for such a voyage. She was of only 370 tons, and many of our vessels to-day are of many more thousands of tons than the *Endeavour* was hundreds. She was heavily built, and carried twenty-two light guns. She was a slow goer, but a good sea-boat, and could ride through a storm in fine style. Cook thought a great deal of this ship, and praised her as "the most proper ship for the service he ever saw." She certainly served him well over many, many thousands of miles of ocean.

Tahiti was safely reached, and the astronomical work carried out. Cook's instructions were that after leaving Tahiti he should proceed to make discoveries in the Southern Pacific. He decided to steer the *Endeavour* for New Zealand, where Tasman had already been. But Tasman had found out nothing as to whether this was a part of a southern continent, or only an island, and how large or how small. He had simply touched New Zealand, and sailed away. Cook took pains to make a full examination; sailing round he found that New Zealand consisted of two large islands. He had trouble with the natives there, and in self-defence his men had a fight that was fatal to some of the too warlike natives. Cook regretted this very much. He hated having to shed blood; and always treated native races with great fairness and kindness, requiring his men to do the same. He succeeded afterwards in making friends with these New Zealand natives, and they became on very good terms.

On leaving New Zealand the *Endeavour* was headed westward; but heavy gales drove her north. These were fortunate gales, for they brought the *Endeavour* off the Australian coast. On April 19, 1770, land was sighted. It was Australia, now visited on the east for the first time. As it was followed up, Cook liked the look of the country, and wrote of it as having "a very agreeable and promising aspect." Fortunately he had come to a better side of Australia than the Dutch had discovered earlier on the west. An opening in the coast-line was noticed, and Cook sailed the *Endeavour* through it into a fine bay, where he cast anchor and landed on April 28, 1770. There some of the crew caught two very large fish called stingrays, their weight was 600 lb. Cook, therefore, named the Bay "Stingray Bay", but afterwards the name was changed to "Botany Bay," on account of the number of plants, Banks and Solander, members of the scientific expedition, found there. As Cook and some of the crew came ashore the blacks met them on the beach in a threatening way. Cook thought it would be kindest to let these naked, ignorant blacks know what weapons the strange white visitors had, so that they would not attempt to fight with their spears and clubs against weapons that could hurt and kill at a long distance. He told his men to fire some small shot at the natives' legs and thus give them a lesson. This was the best thing to do, and saved the blacks from worse consequences. But even after this they came again brandishing and flinging their spears, and it needed a shot from a musket to put them to flight. Cook went into some of their miserable little huts, and took away the spears they had left there, putting beads and ribbon and cloth in their place.

Cook stayed a week in the bay, during which he and Banks and Solander went inland, and were very pleased with the number of strange plants, flowers, and birds they found. Good pasture-land was seen. Cook felt sure that this was a fine country he had discovered, and not at all the miserable place that Dampier had described. Grain, fruit and roots, he said, would flourish in it if they were brought and planted. For the first time some one spoke well of Australia, and time has proved that he was quite right. The *Endeavour* passed out of the bay and was headed up the coast. Just after leaving the bay Cook noticed another opening which he named Port Jackson, after one of the Secretaries of the British Admiralty. But he did not enter it, and so missed seeing Sydney Harbour, one of the very finest harbours in the world. North and still north sailed the *Endeavour*, Cook noticing with pleasure how the country was covered right up to the top of the hills with dark green foliage. He named capes and bays, as he went carefully along, not knowing what reefs and shoals were lying in wait for him. The passage between what is now known as the Great Barrier Reef and the mainland was a dangerous one.

But for thirteen hundred miles along the unknown coast of Australia all went well with the *Endeavour.*

Then the good ship nearly met her end. She was sailing along steadily, when all at once, with a terrific shock, she struck a reef that lay just beneath the water, and then stuck fast on it. The reef broke a hole in the ship and the water came rushing in. Could she get off the reef?—and if she did would she not fill and sink? Cook told his men to throw over-board some of the heaviest material on the ship, and thus lighten her, and give her a chance of floating off. Overboard went six cannons and some heavy chains, with other weighty cargo. The next tide did not float her; but the one after did. The question, however, was, what would happen next? The leaking vessel was steered for the mainland, all the while the sailors working furiously at the pumps. But the water came pouring in, and it was doubtful whether the pumping could keep the ship afloat. Then Cook ordered sails to be passed under her over the hole; and though these did not stop the inrush, they made it less. At last the damaged ship was got into the mouth of the river now marked on the map as the Endeavour River, where she was beached. Then the crew found what a lucky escape they had experienced. As the *Endeavour* struck the reef, punching a hole in her, a piece of the reef had broken off and had stuck fast in the hole. This had acted as a plug, and partly corked it up and but for this the water would have come in so much faster that the ship would certainly have sunk.

Tents were put on shore for the crew. The ship's carpenters and blacksmiths got to work on the damaged hull.

Meanwhile, Banks the botanist, with two dogs from on board, had some kangaroo hunting. After two months the *Endeavour* was ready for sea again, but the perils of the Australian coast were not over. One day the ship was in a passage between two islands, when suddenly the wind dropped and she began to drift towards the rocks. Closer and closer she came; and all on board felt that shipwreck on this distant land awaited them. Then almost at the last moment the wind came up again, filling the loosely hanging sails. The position was saved, but there had been no time to spare. Cook was now able to steer the vessel off from the threatening rocks. In religious recognition of this narrow escape, he called that passage Providence Channel. After rounding Cape York, the north-east corner of Australia, Cook came upon the coast where the Dutch had been, and his discoveries for the time were ended. He was now ready to sail for England again.

Before he left Australia he took formal possession of the eastern part as British territory, which now received the name of New South Wales. He had every right to do this. He was the first comer to that side of Australia and as discoverer he could claim it for his king and country. On August 21, 1770, he landed a party from the ship on a little island, which was named Possession Island; the Union Jack was hoisted a volley was fired; and a whole continent was added that day to the British Empire. Though Cook at the time claimed only part of the country, he was doing more than he knew of; for out of his claim and proclamation on that August 21, 1770 came later the possession of the whole of Australia by the British.

Cook now sailed for Batavia, and did so between New Guinea and Australia. Torres had already done this, but he did not know that Australia existed to the south of his track. Cook therefore proved that Australia and New Guinea were not joined together as the Dutch thought. At Batavia fever broke out on the *Endeavour*, and ten of the crew died. After leaving Batavia the fever again appeared, and was worse than ever on board. Twenty-three, including some of the scientific party, died at sea. At the Cape of Good Hope, fresh food and rest and care on shore saved the others. It was time for them to get home; the long voyage, in hot climates for the most part, had been a very trying one. The gallant *Endeavour*, too, had been at sea quite long enough, and needed to have her rotting sails and cords and weather-beaten fittings renewed.

Cook had been in England only a year when he was put in charge of another expedition. With two ships—the *Resolution* and the *Adventure*—he sailed south again; his purpose being to find out whether there was a great country or continent lying far to the south of the Cape of Good Hope. He was stopped by vast fields of ice, along the edge of which he sailed. He went on to New Zealand and Tahiti once more, and touched at other islands. This voyage took three years. His third voyage was to discover the North-West Passage, as it was called, along the north coast of America. He had for this undertaking his former ship the *Resolution* and another, the *Discovery*. Cook decided to approach the Passage from the western side. He came to Tasmania, finding the natives quite friendly there. New Zealand and Tahiti were visited for the third time. A call was made at the Sandwich Islands, which the Spaniards had discovered long before and which had been quite forgotten. Then Cook sailed north to find the Passage. Like all others who have attempted that task, he failed; not for want of skill or courage, but it could not be done. He returned to the Sandwich Islands, and landed on the largest of them, called Hawaii. There was trouble with the natives, and one day when Cook and some of his men were ashore a serious quarrel took place. The natives attacked with spears and stones. One boat's load of Cook's men got off safely, and he was left standing alone for a few moments waiting for the second boat, which was approaching only a few yards distant. He always thought of the safety of others rather than his own. A native rushed up and stabbed him in the back and Cook fell. Then others rushed on him and repeated the murderous stroke, until the great Captain lay dead on the beach. During the following days attempts were made to recover the body, and at last parts of it were brought by the natives. These were buried, with the sea as a grave; the Resolution firing ten minute-guns. The crews of the ships were too sorrowful to speak. One of them wrote of their grief, and told how they went sadly about their work, not speaking a word. It was Cook's care for his men and not for himself in the hour of danger that led to his death; otherwise he might have escaped. He was a great sailor and a splendid Englishman, and Australia may be looked upon as his monument.

CHAPTER VI

BRITISH SETTLEMENT
IN AUSTRALIA

AFTER Cook had hoisted the British flag on the shores of Australia the British Government took no steps toward making use of the discovery until sixteen years had passed. The War of American Independence had then been fought, and certain of the British Colonies in America had broken away, becoming self-governing, with the title of The United States of America. The Colonists there who had been loyal to Britain, and had fought on her side and not with those who desired to separate from Britain, found themselves in great disfavour and suffering when the war was over. It was necessary to find new homes for them. Joseph Matra, who had been a midshipman with Cook when he discovered the east coast of Australia, suggested to the British Government that New South Wales would be a good place in which to settle the loyal Americans. Banks, who had received a title and was now Sir Joseph Banks, thought so too. There was another difficulty for the British Government to meet after the American Colonies were lost. It was this—prisoners from Britain had been sent to America in large numbers, where they were handed over to work on the plantations almost as slaves; transportation of prisoners to America stopped, of course, when the colonies became independent; and now where were they to be sent? Soon the prisons in Britain were crowded; for in those days men and women were condemned to imprisonment for very small offences. However, though loyal Americans did not come to Australia, it was decided to make a prison settlement there; and Botany Bay was the spot chosen for it. But it was not intended that New South Wales should be for prisoners only. They were to be the beginning of British occupation there; and it was hoped that free settlers would follow.

On May 12, 1787, a fleet of eleven ships left England for Australia with 756 prisoners on board, of whom 192 were women. There were 168 marines with their officers, in charge of the prisoners. Captain Arthur Phillip was in command of the fleet and he was to be Governor of the new colony. The ships bore the following names: (*Sirius*, a gunboat), *Supply, Golden Grove, Borrowdale, Fishburn, Charlotte, Alexander, Scarborough, Friendship, Lady Penrhyn, Prince of Wales.* They were small vessels for so long a voyage and crowded with men and women—over a thousand in all. Captain Phillip must have felt that the hope of all of them reaching the other side of the world was not without overshadowing fears.

It will be interesting to know what Phillip had already done to show his fitness for the new position to which he had been appointed. Here is his story very briefly told. He was born in London in the year 1738. At the age of sixteen he entered the British Navy, and saw plenty of fighting. At the taking of Havanna, in the West Indies, Phillip showed so much coolness and daring that he was advanced by the Admiral to the rank of Lieutenant, and awarded some of the prize-money that was given out. He was then twenty-three years old. At the close of the war, known as the Seven Years' War, Phillip retired from the Navy and settled down to a quiet country life in England. Soon afterwards there was war between Spain and Portugal; he offered his services to Portugal, and was an officer of the Portuguese Navy for a time. But when war broke out between England and France he returned to the service of his own country. Phillip was an excellent officer, and rose to the rank of Commander, and then to that of Captain. His last ship was the *Europe*, carrying forty-two guns. Next came the appointment as Governor of the new colony of New South Wales.

It was a weary voyage for those on board the eleven ships bound for Botany Bay. The ships were closely packed with their freight of prisoners; the heat of the tropics was terrible in the narrow quarters below deck; the food and water became stale and in bad condition through being kept so long; the punishment of prisoners for breaches of discipline were severe. But Phillip was a splendid manager, and did all that was possible for the health of those in his charge. There was little sickness on board; which is really astonishing, considering the difficulties of that long voyage. After two hundred and fifty days at sea the eleven ships cast anchor on January 18, 1788, in the lonely Bay which had seen no white men since Cook left it. What music it was to those on board when the rattle of the chains as they ran out told that the ships were dropping their anchors.

When we read about those prisoners we must bear in mind that it was not meant that they were to be kept in gaols. They were to be used as labourers, workmen, and useful hands, in establishing the new colony. Barracks, store-rooms, and houses had to be built—roads had to be made; forests had to be cut down; and farms started. The best of the prisoners had a good deal of freedom allowed them. The worst of them worked with soldiers carrying loaded guns, on board. Sometimes prisoners tried to escape, but it was of no use; there was nowhere to escape to, except the wild country around where they might die of hunger, or be killed by the blacks. By good conduct prisoners could win more liberty and better treatment; and after a time could get a ticket- of-leave, which allowed them to work for themselves. This settlement made up of prisoners was not a good way of beginning the colony and it never got properly started until free settlers came to it.

Botany Bay had been chosen by the British Government as the site of the first settlement, but Phillip quickly saw that it was not a suitable place. He went to look at Port Jackson, a few miles to the north of the bay, and found that this was a much larger and better harbour, and in every way desirable. He decided at once to take the ships to Port Jackson, and fix the settlement there.

Just two days before the fleet left Botany Bay a surprising sight was presented: two strange ships were seen sailing into the bay. No one had supposed that there were any other ships beside the British in those seas. These two unexpected vessels proved to be flying the French flag; and were the *Boussole* and the *Astrolabe,* under the command of Count de la Perouse on a voyage of discovery. He was as much surprised as Phillip at meeting other ships. He had already been to the Navigator Islands, now called the Samoan Islands; and there in a fight with the natives his ships had lost their two long-boats; and some officers and men had been killed. La Perouse had sailed toward the coast of Australia by chance, and seeing the opening into Botany Bay he had brought his ships in to refit. He stayed there for two months, Phillip and he becoming very good friends.

When the *Boussole* and *Astrolabe* were ready to sail Phillip wished La Perouse and his men "good-bye" and "good-luck," and the French ships were soon out of sight. They were not heard of again for forty years. Then the story of their wreck came to light. It was learned that the two ships struck a reef on the shores of an island in the Pacific. It was a dark and stormy night, and the ships began at once to go to pieces. Most of the two crews were drowned—a few reached land. But when, after many years, a British ship happened to call there, not one of La Perouse's men was living—only pieces of the wreck were seen. A pleasant spot on the shores of Botany Bay is now called La Perouse in honour of the unfortunate French navigator, and a monument has been erected there to his memory.

Phillip sailed his fleet out of Botany Bay and round to Port Jackson; and on January 26, 1788, he stepped ashore at the head of a small cove, into which ran a stream of fresh water. He named it Sydney Cove in honour of Lord Sydney, Secretary of State for the Colonies in the British Government. There went ashore with Phillip the Judge-Advocate, Collins by name, who had been appointed to help him to administer justice, some military officers, a detachment of soldiers under arms, and a number of workmen chosen from among the prisoners. Trees were felled and a clearing made for a camp; tents were set up; a flag-pole was erected in the middle of the clearing; the soldiers were drawn up in line; and a round of cheers was given for the King. Then three volleys were fired, and there in the open forest the new colony was officially founded. The clearing of land, and the building of barracks, gaol, storerooms, houses and huts went on slowly. There were not enough carpenters and builders among the prisoners. Phillip himself lived in a tent for the first three months. It was very necessary to begin at once to grow food for the colony, and it was very disappointing to Phillip to find that there was no one among the prisoners who really understood how to establish a farm. Phillip's butler said he knew something about it, and he was put in charge of a hundred prisoners to get a farm started as best he could.

It was not long before the new settlement met hard times for want of food. It had been expected that in a few months enough food would be grown in the colony itself to meet its needs, and that the few cattle, sheep and pigs that had been brought out would rapidly increase. All but one of the sheep died. The cattled strayed off into the forest and could not be found; though seven years afterwards a large herd of them gone wild was found many miles away. The butler's attempt at farming was not a success. It was evident that the colony could not possibly be self-supporting for some time to come. Meanwhile, a supply ship, the *Guardian*, had been sent from England with stores, but she struck an iceberg, and was so badly damaged that she would have foundered but that a French ship happened to meet her and towed her to Cape Town. There the *Guardian* had bad luck again, being completely wrecked in a hurricane and the stores intended for New South Wales were lost. It would be a long time before any other supply ship could reach the new colony; and Phillip very wisely began at once to make the food that was still on hand go as far as possible. For a time only half the usual quantity was allowed for each one. Then even less was given out: each man getting 2 1/2 lb. of flour, 2 1b. of rice, and 2 lb. of salt pork to last him a week. Governor Phillip shared the same as others, putting his own special stores into the general stock. He went about with a cheerful face, telling all to keep their courage up and hold out, and by and by all would be well.

Phillip did his best to hurry food along to the starving colony. The ship *Sirius* was despatched to England for help, but she was wrecked at Norfolk Island. Just in time to save the colony the little ship *Supply*, which had been sent from Sydney to Batavia, returned with a Dutch ship, both of them laden with food. With great joy the starving colony saw them come up the harbour. Then other vessels arrived, and the fear of starvation passed away.

After this Phillip increased his efforts to develop the colony so that such a desperate experience should not be repeated. He discovered the Hawkesbury River, and soon maize fields were flourishing along its fertile banks. The Governor's farm at Rose Hill became a success under better management. More sheep and cattle were imported, and now began to do well and multiply. Roads were being made from Sydney into the country. Sydney itself was still a very unpretentious little town, its streets by no means free from frequent stumps of trees and logs and deep mud-holes; but it was looking much more like a permanent and cared-for settlement.

Phillip remained as Governor for five years. At the end of that time he was worn and sick with hard work and worry. He took the welfare of the colony very much to heart and never spared himself in any way. One feature of his character deserves to be specially remembered—his kindness to the Australian blacks. He protected them from injury by prisoners and others as far as possible and because of this they gave far less trouble to the colony than they would otherwise have done. On one occasion Phillip went with some attendants and a friendly black named Bennilong to meet the members of his tribe. One of them seemed shy, and afraid of the Governor. Phillip went toward him holding out both hands as a sign that he wanted to make friends. The black did not understand this, and evidently thought that the Governor was going to lay hold of him, so he tossed up a spear from the ground with his foot, catching it in his hand and throwing it at him as he approached. It was nearly being the death of the kindly Governor. The spear struck him just above the collar-bone, and came out on the other side. One of the Governor's men broke off the spear, but could not pull out its barbed head. It had to stay in till the wounded man was taken back to Sydney, where a doctor attended to him. Phillip's men would have fired at once and killed the black who had thrown the spear. But Phillip, in spite of his wound, was as cool as though nothing had happened, and told them not to fire. He said this wild black had acted under a mistake, and in self-defence, believing that he was about to be seized by Phillip's outstretched hands.

On another occasion the Governor came with two boats to a part of the harbour which he named Manly Cove. In one of his dispatches he has told why he gave it that name. He wrote: "The boats in passing near a point of land in the harbour were seen by a number of men, and twenty of them waded into the water unarmed, received what was offered them, and examined the boats with a curiosity which gave me a much higher opinion of them than I had formed from the behaviour of those seen in Captain Cook's voyages, and their confidence and manly behaviour made me give the name of Manly Cove to this place."

What was then a camping and hunting ground for a tribe of blacks is now the greatest holiday spot near Sydney where Phillip's boats were sailed or rowed, across the lonely harbour, there are now crowded passenger steamers coming and going continually, while white-sailed yachts dot the water, speeding swiftly before the wind. The blacks' hunting ground of old times has hundreds of pretty cottages and other residences built upon it. But the place still keeps the name given by Phillip in honour of those manly blacks and is called Manly.

Phillip left the colony in December 1792. He had filled his office most wisely and faithfully. When he reached England he was made a Rear-Admiral, an honour he most fully deserved. He died in 1814—wise, brave, gentle Governor Arthur Phillip.

CHAPTER VII

TROUBLE AND WOOL-GROWING

THE British Government hoped that after a furlough in England, Phillip would return to New South Wales. This, however, was not to be; his service in the colony was finished. In the meantime Major Grose filled the position until another Governor should be appointed. Grose was the commanding officer of the New South Wales Corps, an inferior regiment which had been formed in Great Britain not for fighting, but for police service in New South Wales. He had nothing of Phillip's fine spirit and was not anxious to carry on the great beginning that capable and noble Governor had made. Grose allowed the officers of the corps to become traders, to have more land and more men to work it than they had any right to, and to make money in other improper ways. The trade in rum and other liquors became the special privilege of these officers. They imported rum in large quantities, and then bought farm produce and paid for it with gallons of rum. The more rum there was drunk in the colony, the more money they made. All this was exceedingly bad for the colony. Drunkenness and crime increased; but Grose had appointed the officers of his corps as magistrates, and instead of putting down drunkenness, these military rum-selling magistrates encouraged it.

Grose continued in office for over two years. Then in the year 1795 Captain John Hunter came as second Governor of New South Wales. He had already been in the colony, having come out with Phillip, and had charted Port Jackson and Broken Bay. His orders from the British Government were to put down the trade in rum, and require the officers of the corps to keep within their proper military regulations. They were not at all disposed quietly to give up the trading in which they were making fortunes; and they prepared to defy the new Governor, continuing their shameful business. When Hunter insisted on the surrender of their rum dealing, they gave him all the trouble they could, and got up complaints against him which they sent to the Government in London. They were determined to get rid of him, and they succeeded. Governor Hunter was recalled.

When Hunter came as Governor there were on the ship *Reliance* with him two men, one a midshipman and the other the ship's doctor, who were going to make themselves famous in Australian history and their story will be told in the next chapter.

Captain King followed Captain Hunter as Governor in the year 1800. He also was directed to stop the trading in rum, and succeeded in lessening it. He sent away from the colony 70,000 gallons of spirits, and 30,000 gallons of wine, and in other ways checked the trade. The officers, by way of revenge, did their utmost to annoy him, and to make his work as Governor difficult, or impossible. During his time in the colony there occurred a mutiny among the prisoners. The worst prisoners worked in gangs, with soldiers on guard. One of these gangs was employed at Castle Hill. There were 300 men in it with a very small guard on duty. The prisoners suddenly broke from the guard, and before the few soldiers could do anything, they freed themselves from their chains, and seized some arms which had previously been obtained with great secrecy. Then the mutineers set out for the Hawkesbury River, where other gangs were employed who were to join in the rebellion. On their way they secured any firearms they could find, and also scythes, pitchforks, and other implements that could be used as weapons. They found drink also, and some took too much of it. When Major Johnston heard of the mutiny, he hastily collected as many men of the corps as he could. He could get only twenty men at such short notice, and with this handful he set out in pursuit. He found the mutineers on some rising ground and might very well have hesitated with his twenty men to attack three hundred. However, he and his squad charged into the camp with such dash that, after only a very brief fight, the rebels flung down their arms, and surrendered. The rebellion was short, and it was well that it should have been so; for if it had been better led, and had spread right through the whole of the prisoners, riot and bloodshed would have been widespread in the colony.

Governor King grew weary of his continued struggle with the New South Wales Corps, and resigned his office. He was succeeded by Captain William Bligh, who like all the previous Governors was a Captain in the Navy, not in the Army. Bligh had seen a good deal of service. As a young man he sailed with Captain Cook on his second great voyage. He rose to the rank of Captain, and at the battle of Camperdown commanded the ship *Director*, smashing and capturing the ship of the enemy Admiral. At the battle of Copenhagen he commanded the ship *Glatton*. After that battle, the great Lord Nelson sent for him, and thanked him on the quarter-deck for his good seamanship.

Bligh was best known, however, as Captain of the *Bounty*, and it is as such that he is still chiefly remembered. He was sent in command of this ship to Tahiti, to collect a large number of young bread-fruit trees to be planted in the West Indies. He reached Tahiti safely, and stayed there nearly six months, putting the young trees into pots with soil to keep them alive on the voyage. Tahiti is a very lovely spot, and the sailors of the *Bounty* made great friends with the natives, who fed and feasted them all the time. They liked the place and the people so much that they decided to stay there. One night some of the crew cut the cable that held the *Bounty* at anchor, intending to let her drift ashore and become a wreck. Their plan, however, did not succeed, being found out by some of the officers just in time to save the ship.

The *Bounty* sailed away, but most of the men were still determined to make their homes in Tahiti, and entered into a plot to seize the ship and return to the island. One morning Bligh and his officers found themselves suddenly made prisoners before they had any chance to defend themselves. Next a ship's boat was lowered, and captain and officers, nineteen in all, were forced into it. Then the boat was pushed off and the *Bounty* was headed with cheers from the mutineers for Tahiti. It was an awful position for Bligh and his party, thus turned adrift in a little open boat. The supplies of food and water put on board were very small. Only death from thirst or hunger seemed to lie before them. Bligh determined to sail for the island of Timor, but it was thousands of miles away. What hope for them? He did not know of Phillip's arrival in New South Wales, or he would have steered for the new settlement there.

Day after day they sailed under a blazing sun. The boat was so crowded that no one could lie down to sleep. They met with heavy storms, and so short of food and drink did they become that a half-loaf of dried-up bread divided amongst them all, with two or three teaspoonfuls of water each three times a day, was all that could be allowed. Then they reached a rocky island and caught some birds and gathered their eggs, and found fresh water. After forty-six days they reached Timor, having sailed in their little boat 3600 miles, enduring the greatest hardships and perils.

It was seventeen years after this famous voyage that Captain Bligh was appointed Governor of New South Wales, and arrived to take office in the year 1806. He was the third Governor who came with instructions to put the officers of the New South Wales Corps into their proper place, and prevent them using their positions for trading and money-making. Bligh intended to do this, and soon he and the officers were having a trial of strength. Unfortunately Bligh was a hot headed-man, and often very unwise in what he said and did. He was courageous, and he had right on his side; and he was the sort of man who would never give in. But in several things he did he was to blame. The quarrel between him and the officers got worse and worse. At last the officers determined on a most outrageous act, which shows how lost they were to all military discipline. They determined to surprise and arrest the Governor, make him a prisoner, and put the commanding officer of the corps in his place. One morning a squad of soldiers with fixed bayonets marched to Government House. When it was known that they had come to arrest Bligh, his daughter tried to keep them out with an umbrella! Some of his enemies declared that they found Bligh hiding under a bed. That was not true. The man who had fought bravely in many battles, and sailed an open boat for thousands of miles, was not the sort of man to hide under a bed. In fact he had gone to his room to secure some papers which he did not wish to fall into the hands of his enemies. Bligh was kept a prisoner for some time, and then put on board the ship *Porpoise* on the understanding that he would sail for England. He did not do this but took the *Porpoise* across to Tasmania, where he remained awaiting instructions from the British Government.

The New South Wales Corps had gone too far this time. When news of what the officers of the corps had done reached England, a new Governor, Major Lachlan Macquarie, was sent out. His orders were, first to restore Bligh to his position and all his honours as Governor for twenty-four hours. Major Johnston, the commanding officer of the corps, was to be sent back to England. There he was put on his trial, and condemned to be dismissed from the Army. Other officers of the corps were punished; and shortly afterward the corps was recalled from New South Wales and disbanded. The newly appointed Governor was not able to carry out his directions to restore Bligh as Governor, because, when he arrived in Sydney, Bligh was over in Tasmania. But when Bligh returned to Sydney he was saluted twice by the firing of fourteen guns, was received by a guard of honour, and escorted in state to Government House. He sailed for England, and on his arrival was made a Vice-Admiral.

There was one officer of the New South Wales Corps who did a most excellent thing for Australia. Captain John Macarthur came out with the corps as a Lieutenant. During Major Grose's temporary Governorship, when the officers of the corps were given grants of land, he secured 10,000 acres, where later the town of Camden sprang up. He felt sure that sheep would do well in Australia, and began sheep farming on a large scale. The breed of sheep so far imported into Australia was very poor. Macarthur set about introducing the best breeds it was possible to get. He obtained some from the Cape of Good Hope, some from the King's stud in England, and some Spanish merinos. With these he experimented, soon producing wool that was as good as any in the world. Macarthur did not share in the shameful rum trade. In the year 1804 he had resigned his commission as captain in the corps in order to take up sheep-farming; but he sided with the officers in their quarrels with the three Governors, Hunter, King and Bligh. Macarthur and Bligh at once became enemies. Both were men of furious temper, both were to blame. There can be no excuse for Macarthur taking the side of the rum-seller just because they were brother officers; and he must have known that the Governor was only doing his duty and carrying out his orders in putting down the trade. But Macarthur had very good reasons for bitter complaint against Bligh, who treated him from the first with great injustice. In recognition of his enterprise in wool-growing, Macarthur had obtained a special grant from the British Government of 5000 acres of land. He certainly deserved it. But Bligh objected to this, declaring that the grant had been secured by fraud, and that he would annul the grant. Within a week of Bligh's arrival these two had been engaged in a stand-up quarrel, in which both completely lost their tempers. Then there was trouble over a prisoner, who escaped on a ship of which Macarthur was part owner, the Governor holding him responsible for this. The penalty was £900; which Macarthur refused to pay. The ship was taken possession of by the Governor's orders, until the fine should be paid. Macarthur then ceased to send food on board for the crew; and as there was no food ordered by the Governor the crew was left hungry. The only thing for those on board was to come ashore, which they did. But this was against the law, and again Macarthur was held responsible. He did not appear in court to answer the charge, but sent a letter of explanation.

He was then arrested and brought before the Judge-Advocate, who had with him six military officers as a jury. Macarthur refused to be tried by the Judge-Advocate, whom he regarded as his personal enemy and the six officers supported him in his objection. Bligh then angrily summoned the officers before him to answer for their conduct in supporting Macarthur. The struggle was ended by the arrest of Bligh.

For his share in the arrest Macarthur was summoned to England, and for eight years was not allowed to return to Australia. At the end of that time he came back to his wool-growing. Australia owes much to him. He was the first to discover the great use to which Australia could be put as the "Land of the Golden Fleece." The discovery at once lifted the country into a position of value and importance. He was the pioneer who showed the way in which others have followed, making Australia the greatest wool-producing country in the world.

CHAPTER VIII

BASS AND FLINDERS

WITH Governor Hunter there came in the year 1795 two young men who were to win heroic places in Australian history. They were George Bass, the ship's doctor, and Matthew Flinders, a midshipman. The new land appealed strongly to their love of adventure, and they had no desire to settle down to ordinary life either on sea or land.

They had not been long in Sydney before they decided upon a trip from Port Jackson to Botany Bay and up the river flowing into the bay. Their vessel bore the name of *Tom Thumb*, and was a little cockle-shell affair of only eight feet long. They carried out their plan, and returned with their appetites whetted by this bit of adventure. Again they went to sea in the *Tom Thumb*. A storm drove them south, and when they landed to get water, the blacks gathered about them with unfriendly looks. Bass saw that something must be done to gain their good-will, but the only thing he could think of, was to offer to cut their hair with a pair of scissors, which luckily formed part of their small outfit. The idea pleased the blacks. They had never seen a pair of scissors before, and as the coarse dirty locks of one after another fell under Bass as barber, they entered into the fun of it. In the meantime, Flinders, and the boy who formed the crew, dried the powder which had got damp in the boat. Presently, and while the blacks were still in good humour, they pushed the little vessel off, not sorry to get away from those who might change their pleasant mood at any moment. On the return voyage the *Tom Thumb* fell in with a storm, and was almost swamped again and again by the heavy seas. Bass was at the rudder; Flinders managed the sails; and the boy bailed out the water with which the rampant waves deluged the boat; but it often looked as though the end had come. After an absence of ten days, the gallant *Tom Thumb* and her adventurous navigators entered Port Jackson.

Flinders was now sent for a time on regular naval duty; but Bass secured an open whale boat and a crew of six, with provisions to last six weeks. With these he set out along the south coast again. He discovered Twofold Bay, and after rounding the south-east corner of Australia, he entered the strait which now bears his name, Bass Strait. He examined and named Western Port on the south coast of Australia, and would very much have liked to continue his voyage. He felt sure now that Van Diemen's Land was not joined to Australia, but was an island. Only the failure of provisions and the dangerous condition of the boat, which was leaking badly, prevented him from still proceeding. Unwillingly, he began the return voyage during which the whale boat was many times threatened with destruction by the huge curling seas that broke over her day after day. Bass had followed 600 miles of coast in this whale-boat, and had added much to the geography of Australia.

Very shortly after this, the two chums were together again, to their great delight. They were now sent off to solve the problem of Van Diemen's Land. For this undertaking, they had a small ship, the *Norfolk*. The two would have been glad to go in anything that could float, and the *Norfolk*, though only of twenty tons, was a great advance on the *Tom Thumb* and the whale-boat. Bass and Flinders were now at the work they loved. The *Norfolk* met very bad winds, and was more than once driven back. At last she got round into the great swell and roll of the Southern Ocean. They explored the coast of Van Diemen's Land, and sailed around it; thus proving beyond all doubt that it was an island. Tossing and tumbling, "with sloping mast and dripping prow," the little *Norfolk* was turned north again; and sailed into Port Jackson with another bit of the map of the world accurately filled in.

Bass then visited England and married the sister of his old shipmate, the captain of the *Reliance*. He became part owner of a 140-ton vessel, the *Venus*, and sailed with her to the South Seas as a trader. For a while he was engaged in bringing cargoes of pork from the Society Islands, where pigs were plentiful, to Sydney. Bass's hope was to make enough money to provide a home in the colony for his wife. In a letter to a friend he said: have written to my beloved wife, and do most sincerely lament that we are so far asunder"; and again "Dear Bess talks of seeing me in eighteen months. Alas poor Bess, the when is very uncertain." Alas! indeed; husband and wife never met again. Hoping for better fortune elsewhere he undertook an adventurous trading expedition to South America. What happened there is not very certain, but it appears that he was too daring, and fell into the hands of the Spaniards, who sent him to work as a slave in the silver mines. Let us hope that some kinder end met the heroic ship's doctor, who had a sailor's soul and loved actual seafaring so much better than the quiet medical profession for which he was trained.

Flinders continued to do valuable work in exploring the east coast; but he was specially anxious to get to work on the south coast, where scarcely any survey had yet been made. He went to England to obtain a ship, if possible, for this service. He was granted the *Investigator*, which carried a crew of 88 men. Among the midshipmen was one who afterwards became famous as Sir John Franklin, the great Arctic explorer. Flinders left England for Australia again in July 1801, and began the exploration of the south coast, commencing at Cape Leeuwin. While he was proceeding with his work, he met a French ship, *Le Géographe*, also examining the coast. At that time Britain and France were at war; but there in Australian seas, so far away from the seat of war, Flinders and the French captain, whose name was Baudin, were not disposed to regard each other as enemies. Flinders took care, however, that the guns of the *Investigator* were loaded. He was not going to be taken unawares if the Frenchman meant mischief. There was nothing of the sort and Flinders and

Baudin exchanged friendly visits. The two captains then separated to continue their work.

When Flinders arrived once more in Sydney he found another French ship, *La Naturaliste*, in the harbour; and soon afterwards Baudin arrived with his ship, *Le Géographe*. Governor King treated the French visitors with the greatest kindness. They were many of them sick, through having had for a long time to eat old salt meat without any vegetables. Fresh meat was very scarce in the colony just then; but Governor King ordered that some of the Government cattle, which could badly be spared, should be killed for the sick Frenchmen.

Baudin died on his way back to France. An account of his voyage, with maps, was published, which claimed for Baudin the honour of being the first to examine and chart almost the whole of the south coast of Australia, along which French names appeared, attached to capes and bays and islands. But Flinders had been along that coast before Baudin, with the exception of one short piece of it. Flinders was more than willing, of course, that Baudin should have the honour of that. The French claim in Baudin's name was an unfair one, and has been disallowed.

Having finished his work for the present, Flinders set sail for England, on board the ship *Porpoise*. There were two ships, the *Cato* and the *Bridgewater*, sailing with her. They had been a week on the voyage when at half-past nine one dark night, the look-out man raised the cry so threatening to sailors: "Breakers ahead!" The warning came too late to bring the ship round. She crashed upon a reef, beginning at once to go to pieces, as the great waves bumped her again and again on the rocks. Flinders's first thought was to warn the two other ships. An attempt was made to fire a gun, but the beating of the surf and the bumping of the vessel made it impossible. Before any other singal could be made, the *Cato* also crashed on the reef. Such were the hidden perils of those unknown seas. The *Bridgewater* escaped the reef. Flinders ordered one of the ship's boats to be launched, and going on board himself he sailed toward the *Bridgewater*, whose lights could be seen, to tell the captain of the wreck and the need of help and rescue; but she was standing off and he could not reach her. Meanwhile, blue lights were burnt every half-hour on the *Porpoise*. She was washed constantly by the waves, and the crew could do nothing but hang desperately to the rigging. Sad and shameful to relate, the captain of the *Bridgewater* made no attempt at daybreak to rescue those on board the wrecked *Porpoise* but heartlessly sailed away though he could see the distress signals of the stranded ship. Happily it would be almost impossible to find other instances of such base and unsailor-like conduct among British seamen.

At daybreak those on board the *Porpoise* could see a sand-bank about half a mile away. They succeeded in reaching this by swimming, or floating on broken pieces of the wreck; and got provisions and barrels of water across to the bank. The survivors of the crew of the *Cato* also joined them. They were safe there for a time; but they were 800 miles from Sydney, the nearest place where help could be found; for no vessels were at all likely to pass that way.

Flinders decided to sail for Sydney in one of the small boats of the *Porpoise*. It was a very hazardous attempt to make, but there was no other hope at all: unless help could be obtained it was only a question of time, and all on the sand bank would die of thirst. Again the courage and skill of Flinders succeeded; he reached Sydney, and the relief ships *Rolla* and *Cumberland* were at once dispatched to the scene of the wreck. With great joy and thanksgiving the castaway crews of the *Porpoise* and *Cato* saw these vessels drawing near, watching, as they were daily, with anxious eyes for the glad sight of a sail.

Flinders continued his voyage to England in the *Cumberland*. She was a small vessel of twenty tons only, in very bad condition, and quite unfit to start on such a voyage. Presently she was leaking so much that Flinders was compelled to take her into the harbour at Mauritius for repairs. This island belonged to France; and Britain was at war with France. But Flinders had a special passport as an explorer, and ought to have been quite safe in calling there. The French Governor of the island, De Caen by name, refused, however, to acknowledge Flinders's passport and he was made a prisoner of war. He was kept there for six years. During that time he was often very ill and chafed terribly under his wrongful imprisonment. After a time he was allowed liberty to move here and there on the island; having given his parole, or word of honour, that he would not attempt to escape. Some of the French residents on the island showed him kindness and hospitality, which he did not forget afterwards, but generously repaid.

An American captain happened to come to Mauritius with

his ship during Flinders's detention. He offered Flinders a chance to slip on board, and escape from the island. The offer was refused. Flinders knew that his imprisonment was unjust, as he had a passport; but he had given his word, and would not break it. The American ship sailed away, but not with Flinders on board. Better for him, he felt, to die there than to win freedom by forfeiting his honour. He wrote about this chance of escape. "My honour shall remain unstained, and no captain in His Majesty's Navy shall have cause to blush in calling me a brother officer." That was well and nobly said.

At last, in the year 1810, he was set at liberty. He reached England, worn and broken by sickness, and anxiety concerning his wife, whom he dearly loved. She had waited sick at heart, longing for news of her husband, hoping and fearing. He, too, was enduring the same sadness on her account. Some of his letters to his wife have been kept, and they are full of tender affection. After their long separation they were again united; and though their faces had changed not a little during the many years of absence, their love had not. "Our domestic life is an unvaried line of peace and comfort," wrote Flinders's wife after his return.

Flinders published an account of his voyages. But on the very day that the book came from the printer the noble and gallant writer lay dying. His wife placed the book by his side, and put his hand upon it. Flinders was unconscious and died with the story of his many voyages and discoveries unread and unopened on his bed.

To Flinders is owing very largely the name "Australia."

He did not invent it, it had appeared before his time, but had never come into use. He seized upon it, and urged its adoption, and secured its full recognition as the proper title of the Great South Land.

CHAPTER IX

EXPANSION AND EXPLORATION

WHEN the unfortunate Governor Bligh left the colony, he was succeeded in office by Lieutenant Colonel Macquarie of the 73rd Regiment; the place of the New South Wales Corps being filled at the same time by the new Governor's own regiment. Macquarie would not therefore be hindered as those who went before him had been, by officers who forgot their proper duties, and became sources of trouble and mischief to the colony. He had a clear track before him.

Macquarie proved to be an energetic Governor, and pushed the colony along. His special line was the making of roads, and building of bridges; thus making settlement easy over a larger part of the colony. He found Sydney a town of badly made streets, along which poor and mean-looking houses were placed irregularly. He determined to transform it into a well-laid-out, handsome town of regular streets and imposing buildings. Not only Sydney, but the whole colony came under his ambitious ideas of building and town planning. He travelled a great deal; and wherever he saw what he thought to be a suitable spot for a town, he had it marked out. Churches, schools, barracks, public offices of various kinds, sprang up under the orders of the building Governor. Many of these are still standing with the name of this Governor carved in stone upon them. His name is inscribed freely upon the map, also, in such designations as Macquarie River, Port Macquarie, Macquarie Plains, Lake Macquarie, Macquarie Island, Macquarie Harbour; and in the city of Sydney there are Macquarie Street and Macquarie Place. Well, he deserved all this, for he was a hard-working, capable Governor who did his best for the colony under his charge.

Macquarie was Governor for the long term of twelve years, during which time the population of the colony grew to be more than three times what it was when he came. His human kindness was shown by his efforts to make it possible for released prisoners to turn over a new leaf and lead a decent, honest life. Many of the prisoners had been sent out for what would now be punished very lightly and some were political offenders who were not themselves bad characters at all. He decided to give to all whose sentences had expired a piece of land to be their own property, on which they could settle and start a farm. He helped them in other ways, also, to regain by right living the good name they had formerly lost. His efforts were not always successful; but it was wise and kind to offer such encouragements.

The chief feature of Macquarie's governorship was the great amount of exploration that was done during his term of office. Up to this time the part of New South Wales that was known consisted of only a narrow strip north and south of Sydney, walled in by the Blue Mountains on the west. What kind of country lay beyond—fertile or barren, grassy and well-watered plains or an inland sea – no one could say. The extension of sheep-farming, and the coming of free settlers, made it necessary to enlarge the area of settlement. To climb that wall of mountains on the west was the problem.

For the people of Australia to-day, who need only to take a railway ticket, and get into a train to be carried over these mountains in comfort, the problem does not exist. It was very different when men had to face the twisting gorges with their precipitous sides, and the broken, rugged steeps which sank away before them over dizzy cliffs; and had to do it with pack-horses, and on foot. There are no passes through these mountains; and to find a track across the huge far-spreading jumble of ravines and rocky barriers was a tremendous task. One party after another attempted it and failed; not for want of courage, but because the cruel mountains drove them back in spite of their heroic efforts.

It was during Macquarie's time that these hitherto impassable mountains were crossed by three friends, Gregory Blaxland, William Lawson and William Charles Wentworth, with four attendants and a few pack-horses and several hunting dogs. The expedition set out on May 11, 1813. They struggled up and down the network of ravines, often having to turn back and try another track. In and out of valleys, over breakneck rocks they forced their way; and then, perhaps, came to some tall cliff hundreds of feet high and straight up as the walls of a house. It seemed as though they, too, were going to be beaten. At last they reached the highest point of the mountains, from which the range fell away to the west. On the nineteenth day

Blaxland ascended a hill, and from it could see fine country for pasturage lying in the distance. This peak now bears his name. The Blue Mountains had been mastered. What a sight it was for the bruised, and wearied, and almost hopeless explorers to look upon that promising country beyond. And now, well content, they returned to Sydney with the news.

George W. Evans, Government Surveyor, was sent to follow up the track of the discoverers, and to push on beyond. He did so, and found well-grassed country, and a river which he named the Fish River, on account of the quantity of fish in it. He reached a point ninety-eight miles beyond the furthest camp of Blaxland, Lawson and Wentworth; and then returned. In a very short time he went along the same track again, and going still further discovered two rivers, which he called the Lachlan and the Macquarie, after the Christian name and surname of the Governor.

At once prisoners were set to work to make a road across the mountains. It was a most difficult piece of work. The road had to be cut like a shelf on the steep sides of gorges in some places, from which one would look on to the tops of trees hundreds of feet below. It had to be banked and bridged across gullies; to be carried up steep ascents, and down deep declivities; and to be turned in various directions to avoid great cliffs that blocked the way. A road, a hundred miles in length, was constructed, and formally opened by the delighted Governor, who rode across it with his wife, and founded the city of Bathurst on the other side of the once mysterious Blue Mountains.

Now there arose the question as to where the two rivers, the Lachlan and the Macquarie, flowed to. John Oxley, Surveyor-General, was dispatched to find out. He was accompanied by Allan Cunningham as the King's botanist, Charles Frazer as Colonial botanist, William Parr as mineralogist, and eight others, with horses and supplies. He was away for nineteen weeks and travelled 1200 miles, but he did not find the outlets of the two rivers.

Oxley led another exploring expedition a year later. This time he followed the Macquarie River until it flowed into an immense swamp of reed beds. He thought this swamp must be the edge of an inland sea, which he believed probably existed in the interior of Australia. Turning northward he discovered a very fine stretch of country, naming it the Liverpool Plains. Passing on, he climbed a mountain from which he could see the ocean far away, and therefore called it Mount Seaview. He then discovered a river which he called the Hastings River; and following it to its mouth he named the estuary Port Macquarie. He travelled down the coast to Sydney. But he could not have kept to the coast, only that a boat happened to be found which had been cast up from some wreck or broken away in a storm. With this boat they were able to cross rivers and tidal creeks. They carried the boat overland for this purpose for ninety miles.

The next effort at exploration was directed to the southern part of the colony. Hamilton Hume, who had been born in Australia, was put at the head of an expedition which was to travel overland to the shores of Bass's Strait. Captain Hovell, a retired ship-master, was joined with Hume as co-leader. This was a pity; for Hume was thoroughly accustomed to the country and was a thorough "bushman," while Hovell did not know much about the work he was undertaking, and proved to be a hindrance. Beside the leaders there were six men with horses and supplies.

Not many days after they had started they found themselves on the banks of a flooded river. Hume was equal to the occasion. He ordered the wheels to be taken off the cart; and then with a tarpaulin turned it into a sort of punt. The supplies were placed in it, and Hume with one of the men plunged into the water with a rope attached to them. Then the cart-punt was dragged across, and the expedition gained the other side of the Murrumbidgee River. A strange sight soon met their eyes; and they could hardly believe that what they saw was real and not a dream, when they saw the lofty mountains, now known as the Australian Alps, lifting their summits covered with snow beneath a sky of clearest blue.

A little later another river more difficult than the first was met with. The men did not wish to attempt a crossing. Hovell agreed with them that it could not be done. But Hume was not going to be beaten. The cart had been left behind, owing to the difficulty of getting it over such rough country. He made a rough boat of branches covered with canvas and bullock-hides. The party was taken across in this; the horses swimming behind, held by a rope. Other difficulties and troubles were met, but at last Hume had the joy of reaching the Southern Ocean, probably at Westernport. The party had travelled from its starting-point 670 miles.

On the return journey they met with two very interesting parties of blacks. They approached the first of these unexpectedly. The children were playing happily at hunting and flinging weapons, as they had seen their elders do; and the women were busy making nets, or preparing food. It was quite a pleasant picture. But as soon as they saw the white visitors they vanished into the forest. The second party they met consisted of several men, who after a while made friends, and helped the explorers to find the horses that had strayed to a distance; and also invited them to a corroboree at their camp. Each of the blacks had a good cloak made of opossum skins, and many of them wore necklaces formed of small pieces of yellow reed strung together with bark fibre or hair. Their spears were long and well made. These blacks showed nothing but friendliness to the party of white men.

The explorers returned safely to their starting-point; but the last of the provisions had been divided, the horses were exhausted and footsore, and the explorers themselves were worn, sick and emaciated. They were thankful to have been able to catch a few fish, and shoot an occasional kangaroo, to eke out their failing supplies of food.

The exploration of Australia was going to be costly in human suffering and life. What men endured, and how some of them died, in opening up unknown Australia, we shall read later on.

CHAPTER X

OTHER SETTLEMENTS

THE visit of the French ships led Governor King to occupy Tasmania. The French, probably, had no designs upon it, but King decided to make the British claim to it quite secure by planting a settlement there. While the French ships were still at the Island, he sent Lieutenant Robinson to intimate that he regarded Tasmania as a part of the British possessions in Australia. Robinson decided to do his business thoroughly. He landed a firing party from his little ship the *Cumberland*; the British flag was hoisted, and saluted with a volley and cheers. The French made no objection to this, and probably did not mind at all.

The following year Governor King sent Lieutenant Bowen, with a party of twenty-four prisoners, and six free settlers, to make a beginning in Tasmania. A few weeks later forty-two more prisoners and sixteen soldiers joined them there. At this time, Collins, who had come with Phillip as Judge-Advocate, and had gone back to England, returned to Australia. He brought 300 convicts, a guard of soldiers, and a few free settlers, with orders to land at Port Phillip and found a settlement there. He landed; but the spot chosen happening to be unsuitable for settlement, he was very unfavourably impressed by what he saw of the country. It seemed to him that it would be a huge mistake to attempt to do anything there. He sent a very bad report of it to Governor King, and also said that there were so many blacks of a fierce and dangerous type that he would need a considerable number of soldiers to make the position safe. He asked for permission to leave the spot, and to convey the whole party across to Tasmania. The Governor consented, and Collins crossed over and founded Hobart Town, now known as Hobart, the capital city of Tasmania. The free settlers who had come with him received grants of land, and were allowed a certain number of prisoners as labourers, called assigned servants. In the same year another town was founded in the north of the Island, receiving the name of Launceston, after the town in England where Governor King was born.

Food soon became scarce in the new colony. New South Wales could not send all that was needed; and in order to relieve the situation prisoners were allowed to go hunting kangaroos and other animals, for food. They came into collision with the blacks, and were guilty of vile and cruel outrages upon them. The Tasmanian blacks were specially quiet and inoffensive, and would have given little trouble. But wronged and ill-treated and slaughtered, there came to these tribes the spirit of revenge. They came to regard all whites as enemies, and the innocent suffered as well as the guilty. It was not safe for a white settler to be unarmed or to leave his home defenceless and after taking all precautions murderous attacks were constantly taking place. There was a state of war between blacks and whites and hunting and shooting blacks became an exciting sport; while they in return took their revenge savagely when they got a chance.

When Colonel Arthur came to take charge as Governor he tried to settle this feud by attempting to drive all the blacks into one corner of the Island, where they might live to themselves, leaving the rest of the country to the whites. He ordered a line of soldiers to be formed right across the Island, and these were to drive the blacks before them into the part appointed for them. The attempt failed entirely; the blacks slipped back through the line; and when the drive was over the blacks were behind the soldiers instead of in front of them; the only captures being an old man and a boy.

Then a settler named George Robinson, a bricklayer by trade, a good and brave fellow, who pitied the blacks in their ignorance and suffering, offered to go amongst them as peace-maker. He had become friendly with them long before, and was trusted by them. Alone and unarmed he undertook his mission of peace. He was patient and fearless and kind-hearted. Passing from tribe to tribe he explained to them the folly of attempting to carry on their war against the whites. It took him four years to complete his work. By the end of that time he had been quite successful. All the blacks agreed to go with him to Hobart, and submit to the Governor; but only remnants of the tribes were left to make peace, so many had been killed. Arthur thought it best to send these remaining blacks to some small islands off the north coast of Tasmania, where they could live as they pleased and undisturbed. After a little time there, they were removed to Flinders Island. It was a cold, unsheltered spot; and the black exiles longed for their old tribal hunting and camping grounds. They were not able to settle down to their new home; and the climate made them susceptible to disease, which quickly reduced their number. In a few years all had died and the Tasmanian aborigines ceased to exist as a people. A sad story it is.

Tasmania could make little progress until the sending of prisoners to it was stopped, though it had attracted a large number of free settlers. In the year 1853 the transportation of convicts to Tasmania was discontinued. At the same time it received its present name. The old name, Van Diemen's Land, went with the prison use of the Island, to be wiped out and forgotten as soon as possible. Development came with the fair chance given to this most pleasant little land. Tasmanian sheep produce a very special quality of wool, and sheep-farming is a chief industry. Fruit-growing succeeds particularly well. Tasmanian apples are known all over the world, being exported in enormous quantities; and jam and tinned fruits are manufactured on a very large scale. The Tasmania of to-day is a land of orchards, and with the delightful climate is a popular resort for health-seekers and tourists. The discovery of vast deposits of tin gave the Island fresh impetus in 1871, and it is said to possess the largest tin mine in the world. Gold and other metals also add to its wealth.

An interesting and important use is now being made of the Great Lake which lies high up in the very centre of the Island. Its surface is 3500 feet above sea level, and has an extent of 45 square miles. The water from the lake is taken round on a contour and tipped through pipes over a slope, given a head of over 1100 feet. This power is used for generating electricity very cheaply, which can be transmitted to any part of the Island. This cheap supply will be of great use for manufacturing purposes. The great, silent lake which was a fishing-place for blacks, through how many centuries no one can tell, thus finds a modern use in supplying blazing lights and driving whirring, clattering machinery.

The next separate settlement to be made in Australia was away on the west coast discovered by the Dutch. Again it was fear of the French that led to settlement. A number of prisoners were sent in the year 1826 from Sydney to King George's Sound. This settlement, however, was soon given up. A year later Captain Stirling gave such an excellent report of a river which the Dutch had named the Swan River on account of the number of black swans swimming on it, and of the country around, that it was regarded in England as a very promising spot in which to establish a colony. It was necessary first to declare that side of Australia a British possession; and in the year 1829 Captain Fremantle was sent to hoist the British flag there. A scheme for the colony was formulated in England, and it was confidently expected that in four years there would be a population of 10,000 in the new settlement. It was to be a colony of free settlers, and each immigrant was to have forty acres of land for every £3 he took to the colony. The colonists were to grow cotton, tobacco, sugar and flax, and to raise sheep and cattle. But alas for these rosy dreams! The scheme broke down very badly, and met with failure from the first.

The colonists arrived, and found the soil poor. Instead of fertile land that only needed to be scratched with a plough and sown with seed, in order to yield at once rich harvests, there were dry sandy patches that would grow nothing. Goods from the vessels were piled up on the beach open to the weather. Nobody knew what to do, and no one had any heart to try to make a home in such a place. Sheep and cattle on being let loose ate poisonous native grasses and died. The blacks were threatening and dangerous. Sickness broke out among intended settlers. Altogether it was a most unhappy beginning, with the result that as many as could afford to get away did so as soon as they had opportunity. Thomas Peel, who had been one of the promoters in England, and thoroughly believed in the scheme for the colony, had brought out three hundred labourers, a number of sheep and cattle, and large quantities of farm machinery and implements. He lost all he had, to the value of £50,000. Some of the colonists were not able to leave, and therefore had to stay and make the best of it. The outlook began to brighten somewhat. It was found that there was land in the neighbourhood good for sheep, and that wheat could be grown. Horse-breeding for export to India was established. But Western Australia still remained a poor and struggling colony. In their desperation the colonists asked for prisoners to be sent there; and for twenty years the place became a penal settlement; after which time no more prisoners were sent. The city of Perth and other towns grew up. The interior of the country was explored, and slow progress was made. Then long after came the discovery of gold in 1892. The discoveries were enormously rich, and people came flocking to the colony. In ten years the population rose from 39,000 to 138,000, and quick prosperity followed the long period of stagnation. Two years before the discovery of gold, Western Australia had been raised from the position of a Crown colony to that of a self-governing colony.

One name deserves to be specially remembered in connection with the early history of Western Australia, that of Lieutenant Grey, afterwards known as Sir George Grey. He came out from England to explore the country north of Perth. On his first expedition he was severely wounded by blacks. He led another expedition up the coast in three whaling boats. The boats were smashed and their provisions lost. They then attempted to reach Perth on foot. The whole party was reduced to great weakness, and Grey decided, as the only hope for them, to push on ahead, and send back relief. He made a most heroic effort, travelling 300 miles; just managing to reach Perth when he was himself at the very last stage of deadly exhaustion. Help was sent to the party he had left. All were still alive, except one, a youth named Frederick Smith, who had died of thirst. But all had then been three days without water, and help came only just in time. Grey became later Governor of South Australia; and afterwards Governor of New Zealand, where he won great and honourable renown in making peace with the Maoris after the New Zealand war.

The next separate settlement in Australia was at Port

Phillip on the south coast. Collins, it will be remembered, made a false start there in 1803, and abandoned it. Now, thirty years after Collins's failure, two brothers, Edward and Francis Henty by name, crossed over from Tasmania to Portland Bay. They had been among the hapless immigrants to Western Australia, and had left there for Tasmania. They were prepared, however, to make another venture at a new settlement, and took over with them, sheep, cattle, horses, fruit trees, agricultural seeds, and farm implements. They took, also, boats and harpoons for whaling off the coast. The Hentys, with their households, were the only white inhabitants of that vast south country. Things went very well with them, and they were soon shipping wool, livestock, and whale oil across to Tasmania.

Presently another settler from Tasmania arrived, John Batman, who chose as his home a spot on the shores of Port Phillip. He was greatly pleased with the country around, and wrote, "It is the most beautiful sheep pasture I have ever seen in my life." Batman was a strong, courageous and kindly man. He had helped Robinson in pacifying the poor Tasmanian blacks; and alone and single-handed he had captured a desperate and dangerous bushranger, Brady by name.

Batman soon had sheep and cattle grazing on the beautiful pasture land of which he had written. He proceeded to bargain with the blacks for the purchase of a very large area of this fine land. They knew nothing about selling land. No doubt he did his best to explain to them what it meant; and probably they were no wiser for his explanation. But when he offered them blankets and tomahawks and other articles, they knew that they would like to have them, anyhow. Batman wrote out a deed of sale of 600,000 acres of land, putting into it the names of the chiefs as sellers. Jagajaga, Cooloolock, Bungarie, Yan-yan, Moolookap, Mommarmalar, were the names of the chiefs who made their marks upon the deed as vendors. The blacks received for this huge block of land, 40 pairs of blankets, 30 knives, 42 tomahawks, 40 looking-glasses, 62 pairs of scissors, 250 handkerchiefs, 18 red shirts, 4 flannel jackets, 4 suits of clothes, 150 1b. of flour. Besides these articles paid down, they were to receive a yearly rent in blankets, tomahawks, flour, and other goods. The blacks were delighted with their bargain, and flaunted and feasted in great style. But the British Government refused to admit Batman's right to the land. Of course, it would never have done to allow such a purchase. In that way a man might have gone about among the ignorant blacks, and bought up most of Australia for a few thousands of axes and blankets.

A strange thing happened one day as some of Batman's men were clearing a piece of land. There came along a party of blacks, and with them a very big man, who did not look altogether like a black. In fact, he looked more like a European. He was clothed in a huge kangaroo skin only, and had a long shaggy beard. But in spite of his wild dress and the brown, burnt colour of his skin, he did not seem to belong to a black tribe. One of Batman's men went up to him, and asked, "Who are you?" The strange figure made no reply; but when asked again he pointed to his arm, on which were tattooed the letters W.B. Batman's servant thought that W. might, perhaps, stand for William, and said inquiringly, "William?" Then all at once this wild man of the woods found his tongue, and said, struggling painfully with the words: "W-w-w-ill-i-am B-b-buck-ley."

After listening to the talk of Batman's men, Buckley's language began to come back to him more and more; and presently he was able to tell his tale. He had been one of the prisoners brought to Port Phillip at the time of the first attempt at settlement. When the expedition sailed away, he escaped into the forest, and was left behind. Now for over thirty years he had been living with the blacks. Buckley returned to dwell among his fellow-countrymen. But his long life among the blacks had made him stupid and silent with civilised people. He never told much of his thirty years of native life, though he must have had a strange and interesting tale to tell. He was of some use as a means of communication, and, perhaps, as a peacemaker between settlers and blacks, for which he received £50 a year.

Immediately after Batman came yet another settler from Tasmania, John Pascoe Fawkner. He followed almost in Batman's steps, fixing his home on the Yarra River, where the great city of Melbourne now stands. He had no idea when he set up his roughly built house that he was erecting the first building of a splendid city, and that the gum trees and scrub and open grass-lands where kangaroos grazed would give place to tall and splendid edifices lining crowded streets. But that wonderful transformation was very soon to take place.

CHAPTER XI

STILL OTHER SETTLEMENTS

Fawkner's home became a centre of settlement. Reports of the country around brought others who were seeking their fortunes, and on the look-out for some promising field of adventure. One of Fawkner's men whose spelling was not exact wrote of the extension of the settlement: "People began coming from vandimans land to look at the country, and Mr. Fawkner furnished them with horses to go into the country, always coming by our station, there being no other in the country at that time. Then they went back to vandimans land, and brought sheep and cattle down."

At the end of two years the Governor of New South Wales, Sir Richard Bourke, came on a visit of inspection to the settlement. On March 4, 1837, he arrived on board H.M.S. *Rattlesnake.* He had come to see for himself, and to judge of the future of the place. He ordered the laying out of a town which he named Melbourne, in honour of the British Prime Minister at that time, Lord Melbourne. He also directed the laying out of a town at the mouth of the Yarra River, giving to it the name of Williamstown, after the reigning King, William the Fourth. Then the first sale of town lands was held. The average price it fetched was £80 an acre. This land has been sold since then in small blocks at £1400 a foot. Captain Lonsdale had already been appointed by Governor Bourke as Superintendent of the settlement. The writer with the unusual spelling already quoted, spoke of the rapid growth of the infant city: "There came Capt. Lonsdale with the rattle snake [H.M.S. *Rattlesnake*] slop of war, and two store ships, and soldiers, constables, custom house officers and servants. Then land began selling, building, commenced, then Milburn began to build, then Settlers began coming down from van-dimans land and Sydney, then the country began to flourish, and still doing so, there not being a house where Melburn his now a large City. All this done since i came to it in October 1835, and his still getting larger. I am one of the oldest inhabitants in Port Philip with the expense of Mr. Folkner." So wrote Nathaniel Gosling, who came to the brand-new settlement in the same month as Fawkner. It is interesting to note that he had been one of Wellington's soldiers, a fact of which he was very proud.

At the end of four years Melbourne had a population of 3000. But Collins Street could show very few houses of brick, hardly any of these being of two stories, while there were many spaces in it not built on at all. Rough houses of wood with bark roofs stood where now there are lines of massive and lofty buildings of which any city in the world might be proud. Bourke Street was indicated by a board nailed to a tree, on which was printed, "This is Bourke Street." There were no foot-paths, and after rain the newly marked streets quickly became impassable. Shopkeepers would lay planks on the top of the mud to enable customers to get across to make their purchases.

This part of Australia was now open to settlers, and such fine country at once attracted population. Mitchell, the explorer, had crossed from New South Wales at a new point, making his way to Portland Bay and Port Phillip; and settlers from the New South Wales side began to arrive. Geelong was the next town to be officially founded and so began the long list of prosperous cities and towns that exist in the State of Victoria to-day. Then there came before long the discovery of gold, which brought people flocking in thousands from over the sea to this land of promise. Of this we shall read in another chapter. In the year 1851 this portion of Australia was detached from New South Wales, and made a colony, having a Governor and Parliament of its own, and with the name of the great and good Queen attached to it, Victoria.

We move on now along the south coast to note the foundation of another colony, and the poor beginning of what is now the beautiful city of Adelaide. The colony of South Australia was not started accidentally like Victoria, but like West Australia was carefully planned from the first as a model colony. A company was formed in England to settle this part of Australia, and the idea was that it should start right off with everything complete. Whole families were to go out to it together, father and mother and children, and so complete homes were to be set up. There were to be a certain number of landowners, and a certain number of farm labourers. In the same way the number of tradesmen and mechanics was fixed. Land was not to be made cheap in the colony, as that would make it possible for everybody to get a piece and then, instead of men remaining labourers, they would become landowners and be their own masters. The arrangement was a foolish one, and soon had to be given up. Men who came to a country where there were millions of acres of land to be occupied, were not going to be content for long to be shut out from having a bit of it for their own. This is the fascination of a new country, enough for all, and every man independent; and it was a mistake to attempt to discourage this feeling.

The first new colonists landed on Kangaroo Island in July 1836, but soon moved over to the mainland. There a site was chosen for a town, to which the name of Adelaide was given in honour of the Queen, wife of King William the Fourth. The site was happily chosen, with the Mount Lofty Range showing up finely beyond it. But the masters proved incompetent, and the labourers discontented and rebellious. Instead of going on to the land and getting things started, masters preferred to live in Adelaide, while labourers wanted big wages and could not get work. Soon the condition of the colony was a very unhappy one. Food supplies were imported, none being grown in the colony. The money brought from England became exhausted and nearly everybody got into debt. At last British merchants refused to send out any more goods because the colonists had nothing to pay with. The new colony was bankrupt.

At this crisis there came to the colony as Governor one

of whom we have read in connection with West Australia, Lieutenant Grey, now holding the rank of Captain. Under his strong and capable management, and with help in money from the British Government, the colony rallied from its failure and turned over a new leaf of prosperity. It soon became a great wheat-growing area, exporting to other colonies. But what lifted it to more speedy success was the discovery of huge deposits of lead, silver and copper.

The first discovery was by accident. A teamster was coming down the Mount Lofty Range, and had fastened a log to drag behind his dray as a brake. The dragging log knocked out of the rut a piece of stone that glistened in the sun. The teamster noticed the gleam on it, and picked it up and examined it. It felt very heavy, and he thought it might be valuable, so he took it with him and showed it to a man in Adelaide who understood about minerals. It was a piece of silver and lead ore. Then very large deposits of copper were found at Kapunda and at Burra Burra. The mines opened up a new market close at hand for the farmers. By the year 1851 the population of the colony was over 60,000, and it became one more self-governing Australian colony.

One of the early residents of Adelaide wrote of it as "a wretched village." The village has given place to a particularly elegant and charming city, with all the signs of commercial prosperity. Daughter towns have grown up as centres on the lands where masters would not go to live, nor labourers to work, in the days when the first cut-and-dried plan of a colony was tried.

One other beginning remains to be noticed, on the east coast far north of Sydney. It will be remembered that Captain Cook sailed up this coast in the good old Endeavour, and among the spots he named was Moreton Bay. Flinders came along the same coast later, mapping it carefully. He spent fourteen days at Moreton Bay, and had some interesting dealings with the blacks. He tried to establish friendly relations with them, and in doing so narrowly missed being speared by one of them, though they got on all right afterwards. He has told how, having taken a great fancy to his hat, they made a smart attempt to steal it off his head. Some of them did their best to take his attention by talking and laughing, while another tried to secure the hat on a long stick with a hook at the end of it. He did not succeed, being caught in the act; and his failure was greeted with loud laughter from yet other black onlookers. Flinders gave them some cloth caps, and a pair of black trousers, with which they were highly pleased.

In the year 1823, Oxley the explorer came to Moreton Bay in a small vessel, the *Mermaid*, looking for a suitable spot as a new prison settlement. He found a fine river flowing into the bay, and named it the Brisbane River, after Sir Thomas Brisbane, Governor of New South Wales at that time.

When Oxley cast anchor in Moreton Bay a crowd of blacks gathered on the beach. Among them was a man, taller and lighter coloured than the others, who called out not in blacks' language but in English. He wore no clothes, and was daubed with white and red clay. Who was he? He was one of a party of shipwrecked sailors, belonging to a little vessel with a crew of four, that sailed from Sydney to take on board a cargo of cedar logs down the coast. The vessel met with very bad weather, and was driven far out of its course. The crew did not know at all where they had got to, and finally the boat was wrecked at Moreton Bay. One of the crew had already died at sea of thirst. The other three reached the shore and succeeded in making friends with the blacks. They thought that this spot was south of Sydney, and one of them set off to walk there along the coast, going in the opposite direction to it. He took refuge with another tribe, and two years afterwards turned up again at Moreton Bay. The one who hailed Oxley's *Mermaid* was Thomas Pamphlett. His mate, Finnigan by name, was away that day hunting, but came along a little later and was overjoyed to find a British ship there and a passage to Sydney.

Two years after this a prison settlement was formed at Moreton Bay, but after a little while it was moved to a more suitable site on the Brisbane River. The blacks named the forsaken spot "Humpy Bong," which means "houses that are dead," because of the empty huts left behind. The name is still attached to the place. The prison area was closely guarded, and no free man who was not an official was allowed to come within many miles of it. But at the end of twenty years the prisoners were withdrawn and the district was opened for free settlement.

Allan Cunningham, a great and successful explorer, travelling north from Sydney in 1827, had gone on until he discovered a magnificent stretch of elevated country, which he named the "Darling Downs," lying inland from Moreton Bay;

and on a later expedition he found a pass through broken and rugged country down to the bay. The pass is known as "Cunningham's Gap." Dr. Lang, a Presbyterian clergyman who took a very prominent part in the public affairs of New South Wales, was keenly interested in the newly opened settlement, and secured for it a number of British immigrants. Population grew, the country was developed in sheep and cattle runs, and presently in the new industry of sugar growing. Brisbane ceased to be a town of barracks, gaols and Government offices; and took on brightness, and business, movement, and stir. It is little more than a lifetime since Oxley named the Brisbane River, which till then had floated nothing larger than a bark canoe; and now huge ocean steamers churn its waters into foam. Instead of blacks' *gunyahs* are great buildings and domes and spires and towers massed upon its banks. By the year 1859 this northern settlement had grown and spread sufficiently to become a separate colony, and with the name of Queensland.

Like the other colonies Queensland was found to be very rich in minerals, and specially in gold. Gold has been discovered in many places in Queensland, among them being a spot near the Endeavour River where Captain Cook beached his ship after she had been on the reef. Cook and his men would have been ready to vote the perilous bump on the reef a piece of good luck if it had led to the finding of that gold, and the carrying away of such an unexpected trophy. The discovery of gold had to wait, and when it came it was as strange as a fairy tale. The story of Mount Morgan in Queensland will be found in a later chapter.

CHAPTER XII

TWO GREAT EXPLORERS

ON the daring and splendid roll of Australian explorers, the name of Captain Charles Sturt, of the 39th Regiment, has the foremost place. He did so much exploring; and was as good and gentle as he was resolute and fearless. The blacks were often troublesome and dangerous to him, but Sturt always remembered that they were poor uncivilised and ignorant creatures, not unnaturally looking upon white men as trespassers and enemies. During all his long journeys as an explorer, not a single black's life was taken by Sturt's command. He was able to write when his great exploring work was finished, "My path among savage tribes has been a bloodless one."

On his first expedition in 1828, Sturt discovered the Darling River. His next expedition was for the purpose of tracing the Murrumbidgee River. This river had been discovered in its higher reaches some time before, and Hume and Hovell had crossed it on their journey southward; but no one knew where it flowed to and emptied itself. Sturt set out with a party of eight, taking with him a boat for service on the river. At a point on the Murrumbidgee a dépôt was formed, and the boat was launched with a crew of six. Day after day the party sailed or rowed with the current. On the seventh

day the Murrumbidgee swept into a larger river; and Sturt
and his men looked with astonishment at the noble stream
in which they now found themselves. Sturt named it the
"Murray," not knowing that it was the same river that Hume
and Hovell had crossed at its upper course on their journey
south and had named the "Hume," in honour of the father of
one of those explorers. Sturt decided to follow this river until
he reached its mouth, wherever that might be. When they
had sailed for another week, they noticed at a point where
the river narrowed considerably, that a crowd of blacks had
gathered armed and ready for mischief. There appeared to
be some hundreds of them. It did not seem possible to avoid
a conflict, and, intensely as Sturt disliked bloodshed, he and
his men made ready their fire-arms. But Sturt determined to
delay firing until the last moment, telling his men not to fire
until he had discharged both barrels of his own gun. Then one
of the crew called out that there were blacks coming along
the other bank also. The situation was very critical, and even
with fire-arms it did not appear likely that both parties of
blacks could be safely passed. Fortunately the second arrival
of blacks consisted of some who had made friends with Sturt
higher up the river, and were not going to attack as was
thought on their first appearance. One of these sprang into
the river, and swimming rapidly across approached the armed
crowd, shouting and gesticulating to them, and pushing them
back indignantly as he came within reach. Evidently he was
protesting against any attack on the white men in the boat;
and whatever his arguments may have been, they prevailed.

The threatening spears were lowered. Sturt, ever calm and courageous, landed to meet his friends who had arrived just in the nick of time. The enemy also became friendly, and the boat proceeded on its way.

Sturt went on until the river entered a lake, which he named Lake Alexandrina, after the Princess who later became Queen Victoria. He sailed down the lake until it flowed through shallow and twisting channels into the sea. So shallow and intricate were these channels, and so broken by sandbanks, that the boat could not be got through. The party prepared to return by the way they had come. It had taken them thirty-three days to come down the two rivers; and now it would be rowing not with, but against, the current. It was going to take them seventy-seven days to accomplish the return voyage; and the wonder is that they ever got back at all. Half of the provisions had been used, and it would be necessary to put the crew on very short rations to eke out what was left for the long journey that lay before them. Sturt has told the story of that desperate struggle up the Murray and Murrumbidgee to the dépôt from which the party had started. He wrote, "Our journeys were short, and the head we made against the stream but trifing. The men lost the proper and muscular jerk with which they had once made the waters foam and the oars bend. Their whole bodies swung with an awkward and laboured motion. Their arms appeared to be nerveless, and their faces became haggard, their persons emaciated, and their spirits wholly sank, nature was so completely overcome that, from mere exhaustion, they frequently fell asleep during their painful and almost unceasing exertions." One of the men lost his reason. Sturt used to overhear them saying at night that they would tell him next day that they could row no more. But when the next day came they faced up to it again, struggling against weakness and doing their best. At one point the boat was in great difficulties in attempting to pass up a rapid. The ropes were too short to allow her to be dragged through from the bank; and some of the crew had to get into the water and push. At that moment a number of armed blacks suddenly appeared on the bank. The boat was at their mercy. The blacks rested on their spears and looked on. Then one of them called out, and Sturt recognised his loyal friend who had been so true a champion when the critical affair on the down voyage had occurred at the sandy point crowded with enemy blacks. Help was given by this man and his tribe again. But other blacks not so friendly had been met several times on the voyage; and the danger from them had added to the distress of the journey.

The splendid courage of Sturt and his men was rewarded. The dépôt was reached at last. But it was forsaken, and it was not till help came later that their long-drawn suffering was over. They reached Sydney after seven months' absence. All the party recovered health and strength speedily, except Sturt himself, who bore the marks of those desperate weeks to the end of his life.

After this Sturt took the position of Surveyor-General in the new colony of South Australia, becoming later on Colonial Treasurer, and finally Colonial Secretary. But his passion for exploration was only sleeping, and not dead. At the end of fourteen years he was once again leading an exploring party. His intention was to reach the centre of Australia. The expedition consisted of the leader and fifteen others, with eleven horses, thirty bullocks, two hundred sheep, six dogs, together with a boat and boat-carriage. It was a well-equipped expedition under a wise and experienced leader, but it was going to end in much suffering and complete failure to attain its end.

Sturt followed the line of the Murray and Darling Rivers first, and then struck off toward the Barrier Range, hoping to find beyond it a river flowing from the north-west that would help him along. He was disappointed, and passed on to the Grey Range. There he found himself in the midst of country stricken with awful drought. The summer proved to be hot and dry beyond any that had been previously experienced. He could neither advance nor retreat. The country both before him and behind him had become absolutely waterless. Neither man nor beast could live to cross it. Fortunately, Poole, one of the party, had discovered some rocky basins in a glen containing a good supply of water. This was the salvation of the whole party; and in this glen for six months they sheltered from the awful drought that prevailed on every side. It was a dreary time. The heat was so great that ink dried on the pen before it could be put to paper, lead dropped out of the shrunken and splitting pencils, and the finger-nails of the men became as brittle as glass. Sturt did not submit easily to this detention, but it became quite evident that for a time escape would be impossible. He made heroic attempts to break through the belt of drought, but each time was beaten back by the impenetrable waterless country.

At the end of six months rain fell in torrents. Sturt now set out hopefully for his goal, the centre of Australia. Twice again he was beaten back by country which was still in the grip of drought. He could see before him only endless stretches of hopelessly barren plains and ridges. It was only concern for his men that led Sturt to return. He would have taken all desperate risks for himself; but he did not feel justified in sacrificing others in such a perilous attempt. As it was, the party had become greatly exhausted; and it would be all they could do to hold out until the dépôt was reached again. One of the men has told how Sturt went away alone to make his decision as to what should be done. He sat for some time with his head bowed, and his face covered with his hands. Then he rose and gave the order for the return journey. He had taken with him for this attempt only three picked men, in order to push through quickly. When the little party reached the dépôt, they had travelled 800 miles, and had got within 150 miles of the centre of Australia. Sturt was in the last stages of weakness, and his sight was gone, never to be fully recovered again. He was carried back to Adelaide, and from there returned invalided to England. Sturt was a very wise and skilful explorer, but it was his bad fortune to undertake his expeditions just at a time when the seasons were most unfavourable. Yet he achieved a great deal, and has left a noble name as a brave and kindly soul, an intrepid leader and a humane man.

Another of the early explorers greatly distinguished was Major Mitchell, afterwards Sir Thomas Mitchell, Surveyor-General of New South Wales. His first expedition was the outcome of a story which an escaped prisoner had told about a great river he had seen far up to the north of the colony. This prisoner, George Clarke by name, but better known as "George the Barber," after his escape, had made friends with the blacks, and in an unsettled spot beyond the Liverpool Plains had set up a stockyard which he filled with stolen cattle. He and his black comrades would come down to the nearest cattle stations, and drive away a number of cattle to this hidden dépôt. Clarke turned himself into a black, staining his skin and casting off civilised clothing. But even so far away from British law he was not safe. The blacks themselves betrayed him, probably having found him a cruel and masterful man. When he was taken prisoner again he cast about in his mind for some way to avert the punishment that would come to him. He declared that he had a most valuable secret, that he could tell the authorities of the colony a story of the greatest importance; and the price of his secret and story was to be that he should go scot-free. He stated that up in the north he had seen a noble river, which the blacks called the Kindur. It flowed through splendidly fertile country, and was large and deep enough for the navigation of large vessels. He had followed it himself for a long distance, and it led to the sea on the north coast. Such was his story, and he succeeded in telling it in such a convincing way that an expedition was arranged to test its truth. Clarke did not wait for the result, but managed to saw the irons off his legs, and once more escaped. He was again captured, and would have been hanged, only that just then there came a report from Mitchell telling of a river called the Namoi which suggested that the Kindur might be a reality. Mitchell did not find the Kindur, which was entirely an invention of Clarke, but he did find other rivers of less imposing size than that imaginary one, and vast tracts of valuable country.

Mitchell's second expedition was westward to the Darling River, in order to obtain further knowledge of the country it traversed. It was not a happy expedition. Richard Cunningham had gone with him as botanist, and had wandered from the party in order to collect flowers and plants. He had not intended to get out of touch with the party, but unfortunately he lost his way, and did not return. Search was made for him in vain; though for a fortnight attempts to trace him were made in all directions. Some time afterwards it was found that Cunningham, unable to find his way back to the explorer's camp, and suffering from hunger and thirst, had taken refuge with some blacks by whom he had been murdered. On this journey Mitchell met with blacks who were unusually fierce and dangerous, and a fight occurred in which some native blood was shed, much to Mitchell's regret. He followed the Darling for 300 miles, and settled some important geographical points.

His third expedition was a much happier one, resulting as it did in the opening up of what became later the colony of Victoria. On the first part of the journey he traced the Lachlan

River to its junction with the Murrumbidgee; and went along the Murray, as Sturt had done, until it was joined by the Darling, making sure that it was the Darling, and not some other undiscovered river from elsewhere. Again he had trouble with the blacks, and had to resort to bloodshed. This time they learned the lesson and did not attempt any mischief again. Leaving the Murray the party came upon country with such splendid pasturage, and so delightfully open and meadow-like, that Mitchell went into ecstasies over it. He got a fine view of this great stretch of noble farming or grazing land from a peak which he named "Mount Hope," and wrote of it as an "Eden" and a "Paradise." As he went still further he found magnificent and well-watered lands; and was more and more delighted. He named this newly discovered area "Australia Felix," a title it kept for only a short time. Proceeding still he reached the coast at the mouth of the Glenelg River. He then went on examining the country till he came to Portland Bay. There to his utter surprise he found a little solitary white settlement. It was the home of the two brothers, Edward and Francis Henty, of whose venture he had not heard. To the Hentys the arrival of the expedition was also a surprise, and an alarming one until they learned who the visitors were. As the party was sighted in the distance a four-pounder cannon belonging to the little settlement was made ready and turned upon them. Suspicion was soon changed into hearty welcome; and the Hentys were glad to find themselves thus brought into touch with the outside world. It was a lucky find, too, for Mitchell and his men, for they were able to obtain from the settlement some needed supplies for their return journey.

Mitchell's fourth and last expedition was northward again in an attempt to reach the Gulf of Carpentaria. It proved to be a very arduous journey, and ended in disappointment as far as reaching the gulf was concerned. But important geographical discoveries were made, and the valuable character of large areas was ascertained. Mitchell was fortunate in the seasons he met, as Sturt was unfortunate in this respect. He was specially interested in the habits and customs of the blacks; and in spite of the trouble they gave him again and again he formed a kindly opinion of them.

CHAPTER XIII

FAILURE AND SUCCESS

AMONG Australian explorers one of the most daring, if not the wisest, was Edward John Eyre. After an expedition along the coast west of Spencer's Gulf to Streaky Bay he made an attempt to reach the centre of the continent, an exploit that appealed so strongly to adventurous souls who felt the lure of the unknown. He met with disappointment in one direction after another, and left the story of his failure in the names he gave to two hills: Mount Deception and Mount Disappointment.

Eyre was determined to accomplish something; and now set out to reach West Australia by way of the country lying to the north of the Great Australian Bight. Baffled in several attempts he finally determined to risk everything by travelling along the Bight from Fowler's Bay to Albany, on King George's Sound, a distance of 1500 miles. This tract of country is almost utterly waterless only by digging in sand patches, perhaps a hundred or a hundred and fifty miles apart, can water be found. It was a desperate undertaking, amounting to madness, to attempt to cross such country. Eyre did not propose to take any white man with him to share the frightful risks but a former overseer of his, Baxter by name, insisted on going with him. Three blacks made up the party, with a few horses and sheep, and general supplies. Progress was very slow; all the sheep and most of the provisions had been eaten before half the distance had been covered —he horses suffered terribly from thirst and hunger, and becoming reduced to skin and bone, one by one they died or had to be killed. There were days together when no water could be found—the tiny supply taken to see them through being barely enough to ward off death from thirst. The dews were heavy at night; and Eyre would rise early to gather dewdrops from the stunted little bushes around. He collected them on a sponge, which he squeezed into a mug; and in this way managed to get a few sips of water for the party.

One night a fearful thing happened. Eyre had been asleep, but wakened in order to see that the miserable horses that were left did not stray too far. He had gone after them, when he heard the sound of a gun. He hurried back to the camping-place and was met by the black called Wylie, who cried "Massa, come here, come here." There lay the dead body of the brave and faithful Baxter. The two other blacks had secured one of the guns, and had shot Baxter as he slept. They had then stolen most of the few provisions that were left, and made their escape. Eyre sat sad and broken- hearted by the body of his friend until morning, burying it at daybreak with sorrow too deep for tears. Wylie, one of the blacks, who was an old servant of Eyre's, remained with him; but what hope for these two, almost without food and 600 miles away from any settlement! They set off on their journey again, determined to reach the farthest possible point. Just then Eyre saw from the top of the tall cliffs that make the shores of the Bight what he thought at first must be a trick of his throbbing, weary brain—a ship lying at anchor not far away. Fortunately the ship was real, and not imaginary. He made a smoke signal which was seen from the ship, and a boat came off. The ship proved to be a French whaler. Eyre and Wylie were taken on board and cared for, the captain urging them to accept a passage to safety. Eyre declined the offer, being still determined to finish his journey. With supplies from the ship the two started again for distant Albany, which they reached at last, utterly worn out, both in body and mind, by the sufferings and perils of the journey of 1500 miles.

The story of the explorer Leichhardt is specially remembered, because of the mystery which still gathers about his last expedition. He made one successful journey into the unknown north of Australia; then a second, which was not successful. He set out on a third; and from it neither he nor any one of his party ever returned; nor has any news of what really happened to them ever been obtained.

This last journey of Leichhardt was an attempt in the year 1845 to cross Australia from Moreton Bay, on the east coast, to Swan River, on the west. He had with him five white men, and two blacks, together with 12 horses, 13 mules, 50 bullocks, and 170 goats. They had also supplies of tea, sugar, flour, salt, and other necessary things. The journey would be a long and perilous one at best; but Leichhardt was full of hope and confidence.

He sent a letter from McPherson's station on the Cogoon River, the farthest settlement out west. After that no more was heard of the party, nor from that day to this has any trace of it been found. What happened to the explorer and his men? How was it that no one either black or white escaped to bring some news? Nobody can say what really happened. How far they got, and where they got, is quite unknown. They went off into the lonely interior, and vanished away.

We can only. guess as to what occurred. Most likely they came after a while to a long stretch of dry country where drought had left all the creeks and water-holes empty. Day after day the sun beat down on them with blazing heat, till horses and cattle and goats began to fall and die one by one. The supply of water carried for the men was used up. But each day it was hoped that water would be reached, a vain hope. The sky was watched for rain clouds; surely they would come! If the clouds gathered they gave no rain. First one and then another of the party could go no further, and fell exhausted by the way, until the last man and the last beast had succumbed.

But how was it that the search parties that were presently sent out, and all later explorers in that country, could find no traces of the lost expedition? It may be that after the prolonged drought, there came great floods that swept everything before them, and when the floods went down all that belonged to the expedition lay buried in sand and mud. It has been reported at different times that relics of the expedition have been found, but further examination showed that the finders were mistaken. The mystery still remains, and is not likely now ever to be cleared up.

The story of another disastrous expedition, having special features of sadness, is that of Burke and Wills in 1860. On August 20 of that year an expedition left Melbourne, under the command of Robert O'Hara Burke. Thousands of people gathered to see the expedition start, wishing its members good luck, with much cheering. It made a fine show; for there were fifteen men, twenty-four camels (brought from India for the purpose), and a line of horses and drays with provisions and tents. A Union Jack was presented to Burke, which he was to carry across the continent, and set up on the north coast on the other side of it. A fine young fellow, W. J. Wills, was appointed second in command.

The expedition reached a place called Menindie, on the Darling River; and there Burke left more than half his men, with some of the camels and horses, to form a camp. A man named Wright was placed in charge of the camp, with instructions to follow Burke and Wills, who went on ahead with an advance party. Wright was very negligent, wasting a great deal of time before he made a start. To this careless delay the troubles that came afterwards may be traced.

Burke and his party reached Cooper's Creek, and waited there for Wright, who did not come. Burke, growing weary of the delay, determined to take a still smaller party with him and make a dash for the far north coast. It was a rash plan, and a more experienced explorer would not have attempted it. He took three men only, Wills, Gray and King, with six camels, one horse, and provisions sufficient for three months. The camp at Cooper's Creek was left in charge of a man called Brahe, who was directed to wait three months for their return.

For a while Burke's small party rode the camels and horse; but after a time the animals grew weak and Gray and King walked beside them, while Burke and Wills, carrying rifle and revolver, marched in front. After over six weeks' travelling they came to what they knew must be the shore of the Gulf of Carpentaria, because the water was salt and there was the rise and fall of the tide. They could not get sight of the open sea on account of the thick, wide forest of mangroves along the water's edge. They would have cut their way through this, but were too ill and weak for such heavy work. It was quite evident that they must not delay the return journey; for their food supply was becoming perilously small and their strength was failing; and after a few days they set out. Travelling was a painful thing for them, and the hundreds of weary miles that lay between them and their dépôt camp must have been a sickening thought to them. When they had been a fortnight on the way Gray died.

Two of the camels became too weak to go further. The horse, "Billy," broke down, and it was necessary to shoot him, the little flesh there was on him being used for food. Another camel had to be abandoned. Food was served out in quantities just enough to keep the three men alive. At last they staggered into the camp at Cooper's Creek, and were thunderstruck to find nobody and nothing there. It was a terrible discovery, the blasting of the hope that had so far kept them up.

Wills and King, however, on looking round found a tree with this written on it, "Dig three feet west." They dug, and came upon a box with food and a letter in it. The letter said that Brahe and the others had waited four months, a month longer than Burke had told them, and being ill with scurvy had now started back for the earlier camp on the Darling. What was the date on the letter? It was April 21,—why, the letter was only a few hours old, dated this same day on which the spent and sick and famished men from the Gulf of Carpentaria had arrived. Brahe had only just gone.

Burke decided not to follow Brahe, feeling that it would not be possible to overtake him. And yet he could have done so for Brahe only went eighteen miles that day, and then encamped. Burke determined to take another road, hoping to reach settlement in South Australia. Before his party left Cooper's Creek a letter was written and buried in the hole from which Brahe's letter and box had been taken. Brahe came back a few days afterwards to see if by chance his leader and party had arrived. He did not dig up the letter. He said afterwards the hole was covered up just as he left it, and he was sure no one had touched it. What a pity he did not make surer still, by taking the trouble to dig!

Burke and his two companions never reached South Australia. Hunger and sickness were mastering them. They met some blacks who showed them kindness, giving them native food but the food was too rough for the sick explorers, and Burke and Wills died, leaving written messages full of courage and resignation. King lived with the friendly blacks until a search party found him. The expedition was an unfortunate one from beginning to end. Burke was a man of fine daring and great endurance, though inexperienced as an explorer. Wills was a young man who would have done better than his leader. They were two brave men; and it was a fitting tribute that their bodies should be brought to Melbourne for burial, and that the noble monument which has been erected there should keep their memory green.

It is pleasant to turn from these stories of gallant failure to one of brilliant success, the achievement of John McDouall Stuart. He had been a pupil of a great master of exploration, having served under the brave and chivalrous Sturt. The first expedition with McDouall Stuart in command was for the purpose of exploring the country to the west and north-west of Lake Torrens. It was not a great success. Stuart found himself perplexed and misled by the mirage which created unreal appearances upon the landscape. Dry country was made to look like a splendid sheet of water, and stunted bushes appeared to be forest trees. This made it very difficult for the explorer to judge what really lay before him; for a mirage may deceive the eye to any extent in unknown country. "It was almost as bad as travelling in the dark," wrote Stuart. Truly so; one might just about as well, or better, see nothing, as see what is false and deceptive and not actually there. The expedition covered an irregular track of 1000 miles, and was then compelled to return. Provisions were almost exhausted, and the horses too footsore to travel except in very short stages. Only two meals remained for the last hundred miles;

but fortunately the party came upon numbers of kangaroo mice which often served for a dainty dish.

Stuart did some other exploration, and then made an attempt to cross the continent to the far north coast. He started on March 2, 1860; the party consisting of three men, with thirteen horses and supplies. When they had travelled some distance into the unknown country, a strange formation began to loom ahead, which looked like an ancient castle with a lofty watchtower. It proved to be a most remarkable perpendicular pillar of sand-stone, 100 feet high, standing on a hill. Stuart named it Chambers's Pillar. On April 22 he wrote in his journal: "To-day I find by observation of the sun that I am now encamped in the centre of Australia. I have marked a tree and planted the British flag there." So far all had gone well. Here in the centre of Australia was abundance of grass, and scented flowers, and a growth of wild cucumbers which could be eaten as welcome fresh vegetable. After these difficulties thickened; Stuart fell sick; the blacks became bold and dangerous; attempts to find a way north failed; and it was necessary to return.

This defeat, however, was not final. On January 1, 1861, Stuart again started north with a larger expedition, consisting of twelve men and forty-nine horses, with full supplies. He almost reached his northern goal, but after repeated attempts he had once again to retreat, beaten by a stretch of impassable country. Stuart had made attempt after attempt to cross it; but it was too much for him.

Now a third attempt was made and succeeded. There

came the crowning day of his repeated efforts, when he knew that he might any moment come in sight of the ocean on the north of Australia. He did not tell his men how near they were; but kept the sight as a surprise. They were making their way through thick scrub, when one of the men, Thring by name, suddenly shouted aloud, "The sea! the sea!" and all broke into hurrahs. The continent had been crossed. Stuart stooped to bathe his hands in the water, a happy and thankful man. Presently the Union Jack was hoisted amid cheers from the party; Stuart's initials, "J. McD. S.," were cut on a large tree; and a tin box containing particulars of the expedition was buried at the foot of the tree.

The return journey proved a most trying one, involving much hardship and suffering. Stuart himself became very ill, and toward the end of the journey it was necessary to carry him on a stretcher. He afterwards returned to England, where he received the Gold Medal of the Royal Geographical Society.

The full list of Australian explorers, some more successful than others, but all men of great courage and endurance, would be a long one. Australia has not been opened up without suffering and sacrifice, and there has been no lack of those who were ready to face the risks and pay the cost.

CHAPTER XIV

GOLD

IT was the finding of gold in the year 1851 that made Australia suddenly famous, and brought tens of thousands of people flocking to its shores from other lands. The wonder is that gold was not found much earlier. In fact, it was found earlier, but the find was treated carelessly and forgotten. Shepherds from the country had sometimes brought to Sydney little packets of gold, which they sold there. But it did not seem to occur to anybody that these samples were anything more than chance odds and ends. Perhaps the Government authorities had a truer idea, and suspected that there might be gold in large quantities. But they did not want to follow up the small finds, because they were afraid that the discovery of rich gold deposits would excite the prisoners and make them troublesome when they heard of it. They feared, also, that regular business would be upset by workmen leaving their jobs and rushing off gold-digging. Whatever the Government thought of possible gold in the country they kept it quiet, and were wishful to let it wait for the present.

A man named Edward Hargraves set gold-digging going in Australia. He had come to the country as an immigrant and spent some time on the land beyond the Blue Mountains.

Then he heard of the rich finds of gold in California; and decided to go over there, and try his luck as a gold seeker. His luck was not very good, and he managed to make a living but no fortune. One thing he noticed about the diggings there: that the formations of the rocks were exceedingly like formations he had seen in Australia. Very naturally he asked himself why there should not be gold in Australia as well as in California, when the formations seemed to be the very same. He made up his mind to go back and test this idea.

Hargraves did not keep his idea to himself, but talked about it quite freely to his friends. They laughed at him and told him that he would be merely wasting time in looking for gold in Australia. The proverb says "they laugh best who laugh last." That was going to be true in Hargraves' case. He bought a horse in Sydney, and rode across the Blue Mountains to the district where the formations that he believed might be gold-bearing lay. He reached the inn at Guyong, and arranged for the innkeeper's son to go out with him as guide. The lad knew the streams and gullies all round there, having been accustomed to go out looking for strayed cattle or shooting opossums and wallabies.

As they went along, Hargraves carefully noticed the banks and beds of the creeks; and at last saw what he was looking for. He tied his horse to a tree; took his gold-washing dish, filling it with earth from the bed of the creek where it ran over a floor of rock beneath; and began to wash for gold. He must have been excited and probably his hands trembled so much as they held the dish that the washing was not done very well. But it was done well enough for his purpose. There at the bottom of the dish lay yellow specks. They were gold. He tried again and again, and each time with the same result—gold. Then he let off his pent-up excitement, and turning to his guide he cried in happy jest: "My boy, I shall be a baronet, you will be knighted, and my old horse will be stuffed and put into the British Museum." The district was tested in many other places, and it became evident that a large goldfield had been discovered.

It may be interesting to know how gold-washing in its simplest form is done. It is quite an easy process, quickly learned. You get a proper kind of dish for the purpose, a tin dish with its edges turned inward, and round the inside of it two or three little ridges. Then you put into the dish some of the soil to be washed, and fill up with water. Next you sway the dish up and down, giving it a circular twist at the same time, and throwing a little of the mixed soil and water over the edge. You keep on doing this until there is very little of anything left in the dish; but among this residue there will be the gold (providing there was any in the soil to start with). But how is it the gold is left? Why was it not thrown out with the other stuff? Because gold is very heavy and sinks to the bottom of the dish all the time. The dish is only used for testings and first beginnings—other and quicker processes are used later. But all a man needs to start with on certain goldfields is a pick, a shovel, and a tin dish.

Hargraves went to Sydney with the news of his discovery. Some men would have tried to keep it secret and get all the benefit for themselves; but Hargraves was not that sort of man. The excitement that followed upon his announcement was tremendous. Men thought they saw a sure and quick way of getting rich, and set out straight away hoping to pick up handfuls of gold. Old and young, rich and poor, hurried off, leaving their trades and professions and service. Everybody got the gold-fever. Blacksmiths and carpenters threw down their tools, lawyers and doctors left their clients and patients, teachers shut up their schools, clerks forsook their desks, sailors ran away from their ships, shopkeepers put up their shutters and the road across the Blue Mountains saw a procession of men in all kinds of vehicles, or on horseback, or on foot, making for the diggings.

Other districts in New South Wales were now found to be gold-bearing; while almost at once gold was discovered in Victoria also, and in even richer yields than in New South Wales. At Buninyong valuable finds were made; still bigger finds were made at Ballarat, and in less than a month twenty-five thousand diggers were on that field, and still kept coming at the rate of a hundred a day.

Then gold was found at Castlemaine, and diggers rushed away to this new field. Bendigo followed, richest of all. No wonder that people caught the gold-fever. Tales of marvellous luck and sudden fortunes were told, many of them being quite true. One digger with a single stroke of his pick brought up a nugget weighing 46 ounces. Another took 8 lb. weight of gold out of two tins in one morning. Yet another got 31lb. weight of nuggets, worth £1500, from the bottom of a shallow hole he had sunk with little labour. Large numbers earned £40 or £50 a day, week after week. A black working on a sheep station belonging to a Dr. Kerr came to him one day and said that he could show him "big fellah gold." Kerr went with him and was shown a lump of gold which was found to weigh 106 lb. That sort of thing did not happen very often; but every digger thought there was at least a chance that he might be the next lucky one, and it would happen to him. In one month seven tons of gold valued at £3 lbs. an ounce were got at Ballarat. It is said that a lucky digger rode through the streets of Melbourne on a horse shod with gold. But there were unlucky diggers also and not a few left the goldfields poorer than when they went there.

The discovery of gold made Australia at once a popular country for immigrants, and brought to it what it most wanted, population. For some time immigrants came at the rate of 5000 a week. This, of course, increased the ordinary trade of the country. Farmers got better prices for sheep and cattle and wheat and butter, and storekeepers did more business. Many successful diggers took up wool-growing and cattle-rearing. Unsuccessful ones got work at their old trades; and in such ways Australia entered upon a new era of prosperity.

In more recent years finds of gold quite as rich as those first ones have been made in Queensland and West Australia. The story of Mount Morgan in Queensland is remarkable. This spot was part of a poor cattle-run owned by a man named Gordon. He made a living out of it, but nothing more. Two brothers, Morgan by name, happened to come that way, staying on their journey at Gordon's house. Gordon told them he thought there might be copper in the hills around, as there were green and blue stains upon the rocks. The two Morgans, who knew a good deal about mining, went out to have a look; and were soon convinced that the signs of mineral wealth were good. They took some specimens away; and presently returned and bought Gordon's run for £1 an acre; securing also some adjoining land. The spot turned out to be one of the richest mines in the world. It has yielded many millions of pounds' worth of gold and copper. A busy town of 10,000 people sprang up where Gordon's cattle picked the scanty herbage on the poor land which he was glad to sell at £1 an acre.

In West Australia immense goldfields have been opened up, lying in dry country, where sometimes water was a costly thing to buy, and only to be obtained in small quantities at any price. The difficulty of water supply to this dry area so rich in gold has been met by a wonderful piece of engineering, of which an account will be found in a later chapter. Here are figures that tell the tale of the wealth of the West Australian mines: the value of the gold raised up to the present is £140,000,000.

The early diggings were shallow. The gold was found lying near the surface. Such areas as these have been exhausted, though similar new areas will no doubt be found. Much of the gold now obtained is from a great depth. There is a mine in Bendigo between four and five thousand feet deep. These deep mines require costly workings and machinery, instead of a pick and shovel and a bucket on a rope. Instead of the simple dish or cradle (so called because it was a box on rockers upon which it was kept in motion up and down from side to side, for washing gold), there are to-day steam batteries for crushing the gold-bearing ore and elaborate gold-saving processes in use. There was more excitement in the old days when a couple of men could go out and dig for themselves, and come back to their tent at night to sleep with a good day's find placed for safety in a hollow scooped in the ground under their pillows.

The mineral wealth of Australia is not used up. It is quite certain that new fields will be discovered, and meanwhile the output of gold is many millions yearly from present sources.

CHAPTER XV

FEDERATION

AUSTRALIA is a part of the British Empire; but it is a self-governing part, having power to manage its own affairs and make its own laws. The five colonies of Australia, with the colony of Tasmania, became united or federated into one Commonwealth in 1900. Since that time the title *State* has been used instead of the old title *Colony*. There is a Governor-General, and a Parliament consisting of a House of Representatives and a Senate, representing the whole of Australia and Tasmania. But each State still has a Governor and Parliament of its own, and retains a large amount of independence. One might suppose that the Commonwealth Government would come into conflict with the States Governments, by the one or the other making different or opposing laws. This trouble, however, is guarded against by giving the Commonwealth supreme authority in certain matters, and leaving certain other matters in the hands of each State to please itself.

The Commonwealth Government deals with those affairs which belong to all the States alike, and in which they need to agree for the good of each and all. There are many matters in which it is very necessary that the States should all pull together, instead of acting in opposition or disagreement or jealousy. The States existed side by side, and it was felt that they must not act like foreign countries toward one another, but as members of the same household with common interests and aims, or as partners seeking the general prosperity of the firm. It was quite evident that if some very needful things were to be done, the colonies would have to combine; for no colony was strong enough to accomplish them alone. No single colony could create and support a Navy. Up to the time of Federation the Australian colonies depended entirely upon Great Britain for their defence by sea. The British Government sent ships of war into Australian waters, and did it without any charge. But Australia could neither expect nor desire that Great Britain would continue to do this. The time had come for Australia to look after herself; and when the colonies were federated it was possible to make some provision. An Australian Navy was begun; and now a number of ships have H.M.A.S. before their names: *His Majesty's Australian Ship*. It may be interesting to have the names of these ships: *Australia* (battle cruiser); *Melbourne, Sydney, Encounter, Brisbane* (light cruisers); *Anzac, Huon, Parramatta, Success, Swordsman, Swan, Tasmania, Tattoo, Torrens, Warrego, Yarra* (destroyers); J1, 2, 3, 4, 5, 7 (submarines); *Tingira* (training ship); *Cerberus* (dépôt ship); *Franklin* (tender to R.A.N. College); *Protector, Platypus* (submarine dépôt ships). Of course, these ships of war are a part of the British Navy, as the Australian section of it.

Other matters which have been placed under the control of the Commonwealth Parliament are the military customs— trade with other countries, navigation, quarantine, immigration of foreigners, post and telegraph and telephone service, trade-marks, old age pensions, with many other items. There is also a Federal High Court of Justice, to which appeals can be made from the State Courts.

Each State, however, still retains certain rights over its own more local interests. It manages its own railways, education, police and lands; and can levy certain taxes. It keeps also its own ordinary courts of justice. In many smaller matters a State can do what it considers best for itself, but it must not meddle with what belongs solely to the Commonwealth Government.

Both Commonwealth and States Parliaments are elected by the people, every one who has reached the age of twenty-one and is a British subject having the right to vote. This is an excellent system if the vote is used for the general good of all, and not for unworthy or selfish purposes.

The Government of Australia, as it is to-day, has come into existence little by little, and step by step. When the first colony was founded in Australia all power was of necessity vested in the Governor. There was no other way possible, the colony being made up entirely of officials, soldiers, and prisoners. But when free settlers arrived the conditions became different; and free men did not like to be under the sole authority of an arbitrary or unwise Governor. A Governor such as Captain Bligh made free men angry with his despotic ways. "My will is law," he shouted on one occasion, stamping his foot with rage. That form of government, of course, could not be continued when the Colony became a country of tree-settlers.

The first step toward improving upon this government by one person took place in the year 1823, while Sir Thomas Brisbane was Governor. The British Government appointed a Legislative Council of seven members to advise the Governor on all matters concerning the colony. But if the Governor did not choose to take their advice, he could still do as he liked. The Council had no real power; though a Governor who always ignored the advice of the Council would have been reported to the British Government, which would have asked him for an explanation. At the same time that this Council was appointed, a limited portion of the right of trial by jury was also given to the colony.

Up to this time there had been only one newspaper allowed in the colony, *the Gazette,* published under the direction and control of the Governor. It contained only what the Governor approved, and the colonists, therefore, had no way of airing their protests, or stating their views. The voice of public opinion could not make itself heard. Governor Brisbane gave permission for a free and open newspaper such as the people desired, and the *Australian* was established under the editorship of William Charles Wentworth. Through his paper he raised the cry for full self-government for the colony, and other reforms. All these came, though it took time to secure them. Wentworth is to be remembered as a great leader, and one of the makers of Australia.

In the year 1828 the number of members of the Legislative Council was increased from seven to fifteen, and now the Governor was not to be allowed to make or alter any law without the consent of the Council. The full right of trial by jury was also given. In 1842 the Council was again enlarged from fifteen to thirty-six members; and now twenty-four out of the thirty-six were to be elected by the people. Hitherto they had been appointed partly by the British Government, and partly by the Governor himself.

The final step toward complete self-government was taken in the year 1850. Other colonies had been formed, and now all were asked by the British Government to consult together as to the form and nature of the constitution they desired for themselves. Britain was prepared to give them the largest measure of freedom. It was only for the colonies to decide, and present their claim. They could have all they wished, while remaining still genuine parts of the British Empire, and under the British Crown. Thus freedom and self-government came: a great change from the days of Phillip and his immediate successors, when the Governor, subject to the British Parliament and British Law, was absolute and supreme.

The next step was the gathering together of all the colonies in a Union, or Federation, in the year 1900. Long before this date, Sir Henry Parkes, with the outlook of the great statesman he was, had urged this. For years it was talked about. It became more and more evident that it was a right and most necessary step to take. Then the five colonies of Australia with Tasmania took a vote of their people on the question and Federation was agreed to. The name chosen for the Federated States was *The Commonwealth of Australia*.

The British Parliament gave its consent. Lord Hopetoun was appointed first Governor-General, and on the first day of the year 1901 proclaimed at Sydney the establishment of the Commonwealth. It was a great occasion, gay with decorations and banners and flags and music, with crowded streets and gathered multitudes, and rich with military colour and display, all very different from the first proclamation made upon the spot where Sydney was to be built, when Governor Phillip stood beneath a flag-pole erected in a little clearing in the forest, and the Judge-Advocate read the Governor's Warrant, with only a handful of soldiers and prisoners standing by.

On the 9th of May, 1901, the first Parliament of the Commonwealth was opened in Melbourne. It was opened by the Prince of Wales, now King George the Fifth, and with him the Princess of Wales, now Queen Mary. The Royal Presence was a sign and token of the attachment of the new Commonwealth to the Empire and Throne of Britain. How truly Australia recognises this has been shown in many ways, and most recently by the sending of over 300,000 soldiers, who voluntarily offered their services in the Great War upon which the Empire entered at the call of honour and truth and justice.

CHAPTER XVI

WATER FOR THIRSTY LANDS

IN speaking of the rainfall of Australia it must be remembered that the area of the country is 2,948,366 square miles, or three-fourths the area of Europe, and that it reaches from within the tropics far into the temperate zone. It has therefore great variety of climate. Statements that are quite true about one part of Australia do not apply to other parts; and indeed quite the opposite may be true of them. This is so with regard to the rainfall, which presents very great contrasts. Over very large parts of Australia the rainfall is as much, or more, than is needed, and the land is splendidly fertile. In other parts, chiefly toward the centre of the continent, the rainfall is too small to do more than just keep alive hardy scrub and grasses which can exist with little and occasional moisture. But when, as sometimes happens in such areas, there comes a heavy downpour the country will become a blaze of gorgeous coloured flowers. The scarlet of Sturt's Desert Pea, the yellow and white of Everlasting Flowers, the purple of other Wild Peas, transform monotonous stretches of country into vast carpets of splendour. It was this uncertain rainfall that caused the early explorers, Sturt and Mitchell for instance, to give contradictory accounts of the same district.

The conditions as to rain in which they happened to find it made all the difference.

It has now been discovered that there are in Australia vast reservoirs of water lying deep underground. The water collected in these reservoirs is held down by strata of clay, shale, or other impervious rock, beneath the edges of which it has percolated from higher ground far away. But when a bore is made, cutting through these layers, the imprisoned water rushes up the bore to the surface in an enormous flow, which often shoots high into the air. Such underground reservoirs exist through about half of Queensland, large portions of New South Wales, and parts of South Australia and West Australia. It may be necessary to sink a bore only 500 feet, or perhaps as deep as 5000 feet, to tap the hidden stream. Such tappings are called Artesian, because they were first discovered in the district of Artois in France. An artesian bore in Australia has sent up as much as 4,500,000 gallons daily, and many yield from 1,000,000 to 3,000,000 gallons daily. These immense springs form ponds and small lakes, from which streams are conducted in channels for miles across the country, providing drink for sheep and cattle. The States' Governments have sunk bores in large numbers, owners of great grazing areas have done so for themselves, and smaller landowners sometimes join in bearing the expense of sinking a bore for use in common.

Some artesian waters come up almost boiling hot. This does not matter, as the cooling down only requires a short time. But a serious drawback to the value of artesian waters is that very often they contain a large amount of mineral, which makes them unfit for irrigating crops and orchards and gardens. Instead of nourishing tree and plant life, they destroy it. Such waters may, however, be all right for animals to drink. But in some cases artesian waters are suitable for irrigation, and crops and fruits grow well when fed with them. At Pera Bore in New South Wales is an orchard that has produced the largest and best flavoured oranges possible, for many years. It has been found, too, that certain artesian waters possess curative properties of great value for rheumatism, and similar complaints.

It may be asked whether these underground water supplies will become exhausted as they are drawn upon, and so, little by little, cease to flow. It is not yet known certainly what may happen, but it is believed by those who know best that there is no need to fear such exhaustion. The supply will be kept up by the water that is always filtering down behind the impervious strata.

Another way of irrigating land is by lifting river water, and conducting it over the land in channels and trenches, or letting it spread over the surface, soaking down to the roots of plants and trees. This way of irrigating is a most ancient one, and was in use thousands of years ago in some of the oldest countries in the world. In Australia the trouble is that the rivers mostly run so very low, and some almost or altogether dry up, at the very time when they are most wanted for irrigation. What requires to be done is to prevent their waters running to waste during those parts of the year when they are full, and flowing in a broad and deep current. The period of abundant flow needs to be employed to make up for the period when the river runs slack, and dwindles in its channel. This is being done by building dams and weirs holding back vast quantities of water which would otherwise rush on, and finally be lost in the sea. The water so stored is allowed to flow down at those times when the river would become too shallow to provide water for irrigation.

By far the largest dam in Australia, and one of the biggest in the world, is at Burrinjuck in New South Wales. It is built across the Murrumbidgee River where it leaves the mountains, and sinks down to flow lazily for hundreds of miles across level plains. At this point it passes through a narrow gorge between two steep and almost perpendicular mountains, called Burrinjuck and Black Andrew. It has been twisting and turning through mountainous country for two hundred miles before it emerges between two huge sentinel peaks. Often it has been overshadowed by steep and towering heights, from the tops of which it looks like a thin silver streak. Then it finds its way out of the hill country, and goes placidly onward to join the Murray River at a point six hundred miles distant.

The Burrinjuck Dam is built across from the mountain after which it is named to its twin height, Black Andrew. Nature placed these two mighty columns with a space between ready to receive the enormous block which should stem the river, compelling it to rise higher and higher, flinging its waters back deeper and deeper, and thus flooding the valleys from which it could no longer escape as before. The block has been inserted, and is a solid stone wall, 240 feet high, 752 feet across at its top, and 186 feet thick at its base. What a massive wall it is! And so it needs to be, for it must be immovable whatever pressure may be upon it.

This huge barrier has turned the Murrumbidgee River behind it into a noble lake stretching forty miles back from the Dam. Two tributaries of the Murrumbidgee, the Yass and the Goodradigbee Rivers, are also thrown back in their courses, and for fifteen miles are made into extensive sheets of deep water. Altogether Burrinjuck Dam has created a vast reservoir one and a half times the size of Sydney Harbour and upon this new lake steamers might ply for miles, and holiday seekers spend weeks in exploring its bays.

Two hundred miles below Burrinjuck, near the town of Narandera on the Riverina Plains, there is a very large area now being irrigated from the Murrumbidgee River. Two towns, Leeton and Griffith, have sprung up among fields; and orchards and vineyards, green, pink, red, or purple, with their enormous crops and clustering fruit. Yet before irrigation was employed this spot was quite incapable of any such luxurious growth, or of keeping a fruit tree alive. The water channels, filled whenever necessary, have brought amazing and undreamed-of fertility. This is the beginning of what Burrinjuck will do. It is expected that eventually 356,000 acres will be so irrigated.

There are several other irrigation areas in Australia. One of the earliest of them is at Mildura, in Victoria, on the banks of the Murray River. For many years Mildura tinned and dried fruit has been famous. Enormous peaches and apricots, clustering grapes for raisins and currants, and other luscious crops are grown on land where only a thin coat of grass and scrub, upon which scattered sheep might feed, had previously grown.

Many new areas for irrigation have been chosen; and it is only a matter of time when millions of acres only needing water to make them smile with laden trees, and fields of plenty, will give a happy, healthy, open-air life, and a handsome return for their labour, to a large population. Irrigated lands make a charming landscape, with their masses of green flecked into colours by blossoms and fruit beneath the cloudless blue of the Australian sky.

The Darling River is one of the longest rivers in the world, reckoning with it that part of the Murray River through which it flows into the sea. A most strange river it is: sometimes forming a waterway up and down which small steamers can ply up to a point 1696 miles from the sea; and sometimes overflowing and covering with a shallow flood hundreds of square miles of country; but sometimes, also, not deep enough to float a canoe, or even a toy boat; ceasing to flow at all; the only water along its bed being in reaches and ponds with dry and dusty stretches between.

The Darling receives its waters from the hills along the border of Queensland, and it depends upon the uncertain rainfall, sometimes very heavy, but not at all reliable, of that semi-tropical country. When violent downpours occur there, and continue frequently, the Darling will flow thirty or forty feet deep. Then captains of river steamers seize their chance, and load with supplies for the small towns and the great sheep stations that can be served from the river, returning with their products in bales of wool and other cargo. These captains have to watch carefully as the river begins to fall, and must not delay too long lest they should be left stranded by the shallowing stream. The time for which the river is navigable may, of course, be longer or shorter according to the rainfall on the country in which its tributaries rise.

The Darling is at present left to its ebb and flow, but for years past schemes have been considered for locking it, and in other ways storing up the waters which run to waste in flood-time, but are so badly needed at other times. It is not yet possible to say what methods will be adopted, but it is quite certain that this river, with its long-drawn course of about 2000 miles, is going to be made great use of for the vast areas along its banks.

The question of water supply for some of the great mining towns that have sprung up in dry country rich in minerals has been met by large and costly works. The most remarkable of these is the water supply of the important gold-mining town of Kalgoorlie. A great reservoir has been constructed near Perth, which is fed from the Helena River, in the Darling Range. But Kalgoorlie is 351 miles away from the reservoir, and that long distance is spanned by steel pipes. It is necessary to lift the water again and again in order to give it a flow to Kalgoorlie, which lies higher than the reservoir. There are eight pumping stations at which the water is raised to a higher level, and altogether these pumping stations raise it 1210 feet, and so at last it runs into Kalgoorlie. Any one there who takes a drink or a bath does it with water that left the reservoir, 351 miles away, four weeks before, for it takes the water all that time to get there. When this scheme was first talked of many people said the water would never get to Kalgoorlie at all. They thought that in so long a distance pipes would always be bursting and leaking somewhere or other, and that it could not be made to flow up to Kalgoorlie. But engineers overcame all difficulties, and now for many years water has been carried through these pipes at the rate of about 2,000,000 gallons daily, to Kalgoorlie and other small towns and settlements in that dry back country of West Australia. What a boon it is, the greatest boon that could be given; and what a source of comfort and health to many thousands of people. Thus the battle of that dry country has been fought and won.

The old idea, that while Australia had vast areas suitable for population, yet the greater part of it was fit only for sheep and cattle runs, supporting perhaps one sheep to several acres, and that toward the centre of the continent it was waste land only, has quite disappeared. More and more it is being made evident that Australia was made to be inhabited, and that in parts where a few stockmen and station hands made up the whole population for many square miles, thousands can find healthy, independent occupations and happy homes. What the future population of Australia will be no one, of course, can say. Time alone can tell. A wise and thoughtful estimate puts it at a hundred millions. Some would place it higher. The vast open country calls for population. Those who love a free, open-air life, in which there is room for resourcefulness and endurance, and good prospects of success and reward, will learn the secret of the land that has been solitary too long.

CHAPTER XVII

THEN AND NOW

AUSTRALIA is still a very young country indeed, reckoning from the time of the first settlement. By comparing some of the conditions of the early days of settlement with those that have since taken their place we shall see what great and rapid advances have been made.

In an earlier chapter is an account of some of the journeys of the brave and kindly explorer, Sturt. It was in the year 1828 that he set out with an expedition from Sydney to explore the far west of New South Wales. It took him nearly five months to fight his way to the unknown river which he named the Darling. There had been no rain for some time, and the journey through the dry, sun-burnt country was full of weariness and hardship. Sturt and his party suffered much, and only men strong in body and stout of heart would have held on through the difficult and dreary months.

To-day, one can take a railway ticket in Sydney, and in twenty-two hours step out on to the bank of the Darling River, at the town of Bourke, 511 miles from Sydney. The traveller looking from his railway carriage as he speeds along over the wide-stretching plains may think of the first white men who crossed that country, with only the sun to guide them over the trackless plains, or through the scrub, where it was so easy to lose one's self. The last 120 miles of the present railway to Bourke is as straight as if it had been drawn with a ruler, not a turn or bend in it; but Sturt had to make twists and curves and zigzags in his track continually, in order to find water and the easiest passage for his men and horses. Towns and settlements now mark the explorer's lonely way.

The exploring journeys of McDouall Stuart have already been spoken of, and how, twice beaten back, he finally succeeded in crossing through the centre of Australia from south to north. Along his track of about 2000 miles there now runs a telegraph wire; though for the greater part of that distance the only settlements are a few sheep and cattle stations many days' journey apart.

But for 500 miles of McDouall Stuart's track north from Adelaide there is now a railway. Its terminus inland is at Oodnadatta. Some day it will be carried right through, as the telegraph line has been. If one wishes to travel by rail to Oodnadatta he must take care not to miss his train; for if he does he will have to wait a fortnight before there is another. The time-table does not need to give much space to the Oodnadatta Line with a train only once a fortnight. But this remarkably infrequent service of trains is a thousand times better than none; making as it does a dépôt for all that far-back country, and taking the place of the horse or bullock teams which needed weeks or months to cover the distance over which the railway runs.

An interesting little railway, 150 miles in length, has been constructed from Darwin on the north coast into the interior. This will be connected with Oodnadatta on the southern side of Central Australia, when the railway through the continent from north to south is built, as promised by the Commonwealth Agreement. Darwin is the port and chief town of what is called the Northern Territory, and possesses a very fine and spacious harbour. There is very little population as yet in the Northern Territory, though much of it is rich and fertile country. The reason that little settlement has taken place is chiefly because this extreme north of Australia is very hot, and therefore trying to white people. It is, however, no hotter than many other parts of the world where white people live; and many of those who have settled in the Northern Territory say it is quite healthy. The railway from Darwin runs into the Bush, passing at times through thick jungle, with just enough space on each side of the line to keep the engine and carriages or trucks clear of the luxuriant tropical growth. Often the line is hemmed in by magnificent trees and palms and shrubs and creepers, which form for it a lovely avenue. The train from Darwin to the terminus at Pine Creek lying 150 miles inland is not in a great hurry. It has no need to get out of the way of other trains; for it has the line from beginning to end all to itself. Passengers by it are very few. One car is sufficient for them, the rest of the train being made up of goods wagons. The guard of the train is also a postman; and the train stops here and there while he gets down and puts letters and papers and parcels into the boxes that are nailed to trees at certain points. Settlers come from long distances to empty the boxes, or perhaps are waiting for the train when it arrives. Flocks of birds go off noisily as the engine comes puffing along; and every now and then a wallaby or kangaroo hops across the line; or a group of blacks from their camp near by may be seen and heard, holding out their hands and calling for tobacco and food. The guard, being a handy man, will make tea with hot water from the engine for the few passengers on board the train. So this Bush train, which is no express, makes its own time-table as it goes along, and arrives sooner or later at its destination.

There are many railways running far back into the country, where sheep and cattle stations and farmsteads may be so far apart that people have to travel very many miles to see their nearest neighbour; or where mining settlements have sprung up far away from the older and more populated districts. Huge wagons, drawn by teams of twenty or thirty bullocks, or ten or twelve horses, will carry wool to the nearest railway station; and sheep and cattle will be driven there, to be put into trucks for distant markets. It may still be a very long journey, taking several days or even weeks, in order to reach the railway, but every line running back into the country makes it easier for settlers to send away what they have to sell, get the supplies they need, and take a trip themselves either for business or pleasure. The telephone and motor-car, too, are now a very great boon to distant settlers. A telephone wire is often run, for scores of miles, along the top of the fences that enclose the huge paddocks, thousands of acres in extent. In Queensland, one line from Brisbane runs inland to Cunnamulla, 694 miles;

another from Rockhampton on the coast runs back to Long-reach, 428 miles; another from the port of Townsville back to Dajarra, 582 miles; and other similar lines. In all the States, railways connect the country inland with the various ports; and such lines are constantly being increased in length and numbers. In the more thickly populated districts railways lie much closer together, becoming a close network in certain parts. As compared with one train a fortnight to Oodnadatta there are altogether 755 passenger trains going in and out of the Central Railway Station in Sydney every day.

One line of railway that has recently been completed deserves special notice. It is known as the East-West Transcontinental Railway, because it joins the east and west sides of Australia. For a long time past Queensland, New South Wales, Victoria and South Australia have been linked together by railways; but there was a great space separating these States from Western Australia. The space that needed to be crossed by a railway in order to join up Western Australia was 1051 miles, from Port Augusta to Kalgoorlie. That blank has now been filled.

In building the East-West Railway the greatest difficulty was want of water along the route. That part of Australia lying north of the Great Australian Bight is particularly waterless; and how to supply the large number of workmen with water for all purposes was a serious problem. For the health and comfort of the men larger supplies were needed than it was possible to carry over such long distances. Along the route water could be obtained at many points by sinking wells and putting down bores, but frequently the water got in that way proved to be salt. There were some shallow lakes along the track but they were salt—one of them, Lake Windabout, being three times salter than the sea. These lakes often dry up, and then salt can be scraped up in heaps along their beds. Some wells and bores, however, turned out all right, yielding good fresh water; and by condensation fresh water was obtained from the salt sources.

The line was laid piece by piece. As soon as a stretch was ready for the rails, they were laid; and an engine with trucks of food, water tanks, a hospital van, and other necessary supplies was run along the newly laid rails, following up the workmen as closely as possible. Those who had to go still further ahead, preparing the line, were catered for by camel teams.

It took five years to build the East-West Transcontinental Railway, and the cost has been about £7,500,000. It may be asked why so much money was spent in making a rail- way through this dry country, where for a stretch of 700 miles there was not a single white inhabitant. The answer is that this railway joins all the more populated parts of Australia together as one whole and it might be needed some day for military purposes, though everybody hopes it will not. This rail-way enables a quicker delivery to the southern and eastern States of letters from Great Britain and other lands, and also shortens the journey for passengers, by cutting out the neces- sity of the voyage across the Great Bight,—railway travelling being so much faster than sea travelling. It is now possible to travel by rail from Longreach in Queensland, on the east coast, to Perth, on the west coast, a distance of 4300 miles.

One of the passengers by the first through train from Perth to Port Augusta and Adelaide over the new line was Lord Forrest, a great Australian statesman. When he was a young man, and had no title, he did some most valuable exploring in Western Australia, with his brother, Alexander Forrest. Once in those days he was wounded by blacks. Lord Forrest and his brother, with a very small party, were the first to cross the difficult country which the East-West Railway now traverses. Several times on that exploring journey the whole party was at the point of death from thirst. No wonder that Lord Forrest, as he sat at ease in a comfortable railway carriage, thought of that journey of years ago which more than once nearly cost him his life: where he and his party vainly sought for enough water to quench their awful thirst, now iced drinks or tea or coffee could be called for in the pleasant dining-saloon of the train: where he had slept on the ground with his horse's saddle for a pillow, now he had a soft bed in a sleeping-car. Where it had taken him 142 hard, weary days to cross that stretch of country on his exploring journey, now he could cross it in ease and comfort in two and a half days.

Another instance of change recalls once more the name of Sturt. In his attempt to reach the centre of the continent he crossed a range of hills known as the Barrier Range. If any one had told Sturt that those rough, sun-baked hills held so much mineral wealth that millions of pounds would be dug out of them, and that a fine town of thirty thousand people would spring up on their dry slopes, he would have thought it a mad idea. But it would have been quite true. There is to-day on the Barrier Range a great mining town, and scores of millions of pounds' worth of minerals have been taken out of the hills that Sturt thought worthless.

The city of Broken Hill has sprung up there, so named from the shape of the rugged hill around which it is built. It was a stock-man, Paddy Ryan, who first found silver on the Barrier Range, as he rode across looking for strayed cattle. The news went abroad, and a large number of men were soon on the spot, hoping to make their fortunes quickly. They were disappointed, and went away. But other silver lodes were found, and a town came into existence, to which the name of Silverton was given. It reached a population of 3000, but did not last long. It was forsaken, and many of its houses were removed to a new town that was being formed not far away.

As Silverton failed mineral discoveries were made at a spot marked by a curiously shaped hill which was soon known as "The Broken Hill." There, not only silver, but also exceedingly rich zinc-lead-sulphide ore was found. The town of Broken Hill grew up quickly around the valuable mines that were opened up. To-day, the once silent hills resound with the clatter of machinery, and the heavy rattling thud of the huge batteries that pound the ore to powder. At night the hill-sides are ablaze with electric lights around the mines; for work goes on day and night alike. Broken Hill is a busy place, with electric trams in its streets, a fine water supply brought from a distance, churches, schools, banks, stores, public library, hospitals, newspapers of its own, and all the signs of a rich and prosperous town. A railway links it to Port Pirie and Adelaide. The Broken Hill Proprietary Mine is not only the largest mine in Australia, but also the largest in the world; and it is only one of the mines in that rich area.

The coalfields of Australia are immense. Coal was discovered very early in the history of settlement. A ship had been wrecked on the Furneaux Group of islands, and the cast-away sailors managed to reach the east coast of Australia in one of the ship's boats. They then set out to walk along the coast to Sydney, a distance of 300 miles, which only three of them lived to reach. On their way they noticed coal lying on the beach at a certain spot. They reported this in Sydney, and in consequence of their story, Bass, one of the heroes of the *Tom Thumb* and the *Norfolk*, was sent down the coast to examine the spot. He found in the lofty cliff at this point a seam of coal six feet thick, from which the coal on the beach had fallen. Coal was found later also north of Sydney, where the Hunter River enters the sea. Since then yet other coalfields have been discovered.

Where the shipwrecked sailors saw the coal on the beach, and Bass looked up to see the seam in the cliff, there are now vast coal-pits, and steamers lying alongside great jetties on to which long trains of coal-trucks are run to be tipped into the vessels by thousands of tons continually. At the mouth of the Hunter River the great port of Newcastle has grown up, with forests of masts and funnels belonging to sailing ships and steamers loading coal for far-off lands in Asia and America.

Such are a few of the many vivid contrasts between the early days that are so recent, and the present. But the greatest contrast between then and now has been brought about by the transformation of forest, bush and scrub into vast pastoral areas, wheat-fields, sugar plantations, orchards and vineyards, dotted with beautiful and comfortable dwellings, thriving towns, and smaller centres of settlement. In Australia there are 86,000,000 sheep yielding more than 632,000,000 lb. of wool yearly, 12,000,000 cattle, 9,300,000 acres of wheat, beside other important branches of farming. But Australia has lands and homes to offer still to multitudes who will accept her offers of welcome.

One very different contrast needs still to be mentioned. The Great War suddenly transformed Australia into a military country. That story is too great to be told here, a story of deathless fame. From this new land at the call of King and Empire and Duty, and for the sake of Justice and Freedom and Civilisation, more than 400,000 men voluntarily responded. The military force of the early days was about 180 marines, who came out with Phillip as prisoners' guards. Now Australia can send her own soldiers by hundreds of thousands to fight by the side of those from the Motherland and from all parts of the Empire. In the year 1788 the little gunboat *Sirius*, with tall masts and spreading sales, tacked up Sydney Harbour, the waters of which till then had never been rippled by the prow of a larger vessel than an aboriginal's bark canoe. Then the shores were clothed in the dark green foliage of unbroken bush, and all was so lonely and silent that it might have been without a single inhabitant. What few wild inhabitants there were hid themselves among the trees, and peered out upon the strange sight of the sailing ships that alarmed them. Phillip saw that the harbour was wonderful in size and beauty, but his wildest dreams could not have pictured what it was to become. Sydney now ranks as the fifth port of the British Empire in the amount of shipping that comes and goes to and from it. From the lonely harbour into which Phillip sailed there have departed during the Great War transport after transport, great vessels that would have overshadowed the *Sirius* and made it look very tiny indeed, crowded with troops eager to serve, and ready to suffer and die. From Melbourne, Brisbane, Perth and Hobart the same gallant departures have been seen. This is the latest sign and proof of the fitness and truth of the Australian motto –

"ADVANCE AUSTRALIA."

CHAPTER XVIII

THE BUSH: ITS TREES AND FLOWERS

"THE BUSH" is the name given in Australia to native vegetation in forest, or scrub, or brushland; and it is often used in a general sense for any part of the country that has not been brought into use for pasture or cultivation. The Bush is thickest and tallest near the coast, and becomes sparse and shorter as it lies farther inland, because the rainfall of Australia is less and less as the interior is reached.

The tree that specially belongs to Australia and may be called the national tree is the Gum Tree. It was so named by the first settlers in Australia because of a sticky red substance that oozed from its bark and looked like gum. It is not really gum at all, but what chemists call a *kino*, and it is used for medicinal purposes. The scientific name for the so-called gum tree is Eucalyptus, but the old rough-and-ready name is mostly used. The word Eucalyptus means "well covered," and is made from two Greek words. This name is given because parts of the flowers of the tree are specially protected by a cover, or operculum. The eucalyptus is not just one kind of tree, but is the name of a large family made up of many classes.

There are about two hundred different kinds of eucalyptus, all related to one another, and known all together as Eucalypts.

Some Eucalypts grow to a very great height, over 300 feet; and for 100 feet or more the trunk of the tree will be quite bare, not sending out a single branch or twig. Eucalypts grow very quickly, even as much as ten feet in a year. Some of them will increase in size as much in twenty-four years as an English oak would do in two hundred years. There will often be enough timber in a single gum tree to build a five-roomed wooden cottage—walls, floors, ceiling, roof, joists, all complete. Mueller declared that one blue gum he saw "contained as much timber as would fully suffice to build a 90-ton schooner."

Settlers in Australia soon began to name Eucalypts after the sort of bark that covered them, such as white gum, blue gum, spotted gum, stringy bark, iron bark, blood wood (because of the large quantity of red kino that ran out of it), and others beside. Then they found the timber, or leaves, of some of them rather like those of trees they had known in the old country from which they had come on the other side of the world. So they gave the names of those trees in the old home lands to trees in the new land of Australia, such as ash, apple, box, and elm. One they called mahogany, because of its timber being like the Spanish or Honduras mahogany, of which much of the household furniture they had been accustomed to was made. Another they called the peppermint, and were glad to find, too, that a medicine could be made from these leaves as good as the peppermint of the old country.

Those first settlers quickly noticed two peculiar things about the Eucalypts. First, that some shed their bark, and not their leaves like the trees they had been used to; next, that the Eucalypts turned the narrow edges of their leaves, instead of their flat surfaces, to the sun, and so did not give much shade. On a bright hot day Eucalypts do not cast a heavy shadow. Their leaves turned edge-ways to the sun make only a poor protection from its blaze, which strikes down between them.

As Eucalypts have become better known they have been found to be most valuable trees, and among the very best in the world. Their home is in Australia, but they have now been planted in many other countries in Europe, Asia, Africa and America, where they grow well. The planting of Eucalypts, specially certain kinds, in unhealthy parts of some of these countries, has done a great deal of good in lessening the fevers that used to be common in those parts.

Almost every portion of many Eucalypts is quite valuable— leaves, flowers, bark, and timber. The leaves give an oil that is very good as a medicine, and is used in this way all over the world. The leaves of some yield an oil which is used in making perfumes, and, strange as it may seem, there can be made from them a scent just like that of violets, or like the costly scent known as Attar of Roses. Another gives an oil that is used in separating certain minerals. This is done by what is called flotation; the oil is mixed with the earth, which contains very small particles of mineral such as silver or lead, and with water. The oil then makes bubbles which float on the top of the mixture, gathering and holding in them the particles of silver, or other mineral. The oil and mineral are then skimmed off the top and separated from one another. The leaves of some stringy bark Eucalypts yield turpentine, which is just the same as that got from pine trees in Europe and America.

The flowers of Eucalypts provide honey for bees; and bees will gather from them many tons of honey, which is afterwards taken from the hives for home use or sent to market by the bee-keepers. All Eucalypts do not flower at the same time, so that bees are able to gather first from the earlier flowering kinds, and then from later ones in turn, and thus get many harvests in a year.

The bark of certain Eucalypts, specially the stringy bark, was soon found to be very useful for house-building. The first settlers had to put up their homes as quickly as possible, and it was a great thing for them to be able to strip the bark off these trees and use it for rough walls and roofs. The bark can be taken off in long, wide sheets and then flattened out. Fastened on to a frame-work of poles it makes a good covering from sun or wind or rain. Bark is still used in this way for miners' huts or sheds, or other farm buildings in the Bush.

The timber of Eucalypts is among the hardest, best wearing timber in the world. Some Eucalypts are exceedingly tough, and, like English oak, will last for a very long time; and because of their great size, huge beams can be sawn out of them. Timber from Eucalypts is used for the immense girders of bridges and wharves; for tall piles driven into the beds of rivers and harbours, where they will not rot beneath the water for very many years—for joists of roofs and floors of buildings; for railway trucks and carriages; for street-paving blocks—for furniture; and for many other purposes.

These timbers are not only tough and lasting, but also very beautiful when polished; and are of many shades. A set of polished Eucalypt boards would show rich browns and reds and yellows, varying from dark to light, and suitable for all kinds of ornamental work.

There are thinner and shorter Eucalypts that are not found growing in the tall, dense bush along the coasts, but in the drier back country. These are called Mallees. A peculiar thing about them is that they do not grow with one trunk or stem, but with several stems spreading upwards from the ground. Much more peculiar are the roots of some of these mallees, in the way they hold water. The blacks found this out; and where water cannot be got in the ordinary way, they will pull up a root of the right kind of mallee, chop it into short pieces, and holding up a piece let the water from it drop into their mouths, getting quite a good drink.

Another kind of drinking-fountain tree is the Bottle Tree, which grows chiefly in Queensland and Western Australia. It gets its name partly from the shape of its stem, which is rather like a bottle with the branches growing out of the bottle neck, and also because it holds a great deal of fluid, which makes a pleasant drink. The wood is very soft, and when a hole is cut in the side of the tree the fluid oozes out and the tree becomes a drinking fountain.

Though Australia is the land of the Eucalypts, there are

many other large and useful trees in it. The Red Cedar grows to a tremendous size, and has a rich colouring which makes it a very fine timber for furniture and house fittings. Pines grow to a very great height. Red bean, black bean (or Moreton Bay chestnut), white beech, tulip wood and other trees are valuable for many purposes. Sandalwood grows in West Australia and in Queensland. Though great areas of forest have been cleared for grazing land and farms, and millions upon millions of splendid trees have been burnt to make room for pastures and crops, there are still vast forests in Australia, and many of them are being kept as forest reserves by the Governments of the States.

The ferns of the Bush are of many beautiful kinds. The greatest of them is the Tree Fern. It grows very tall, with a straight stem, from the top of which spreads out a perfect circle of fronds, perhaps ten feet in length. One can walk under them as they make a roof of graceful arching green, while through chinks in the fronds there fall little blobs of sunshine on to the ground beneath; and the green of the roof is mixed with the gold of the sunshine and the blue of the sky.

The Grass Tree is a curious-looking growth. It has a long stem like the fern tree, but instead of long arching fronds it has a big tuft of thin wiry leaves that look like grass growing out of it, and hanging round as though it were a mob of hair that needed combing. Out of this mob there springs a long stalk, standing up like a spear, and bearing white flowers in season.

The flowers of Australia are abundant and different from

those in other parts of the world. Even in the very dry interior, where at times it seems as though nearly everything had died away for want of rain, when the rain does come at last, flowers spring up and make the country lovely for a while with their bloom. The strangeness of Australian trees and plants and flowers, so different from all other lands, greatly delighted Joseph Banks, the botanist travelling with Captain Cook, and led to the calling of the place in which he first found these new and remarkable, specimens, Botany Bay.

There is one common mistake about Australian flowers which needs to be put right. It has often been said that they have no scent. Certainly, some of them have not, but very many have a sweet and delicate perfume; and to make up for those that have none, the leaves are scented instead of the flowers in many cases. Australia is, indeed, the home of the scented trees and shrubs, and the sweet smell of the Bush fills the air right through it.

Among the flowering shrubs, the best known is the Wattle. The Wattle Blossom has been chosen as the national flower of Australia in the same way that the rose is the national flower of England, or the lily of France. There are a great many varieties of wattle, some being small shrubs and some fair-sized trees. In their season they are covered with golden bloom of lighter or darker shades. When growing together in great numbers, every branch and twig hung with the glowing yellow blossoms and caught at every tip by the glorious sunshine, they look like banks of gold set up against the blue sky.

Among the flowering trees, of which there are so many,

the Flame Tree of New South Wales is one of the most striking. Its great red blooms can be seen on a hill-side from miles away, as though they were flames breaking from the tree. The Fire Tree in West Australia in the same way blazes with orange-coloured bloom like a tree on fire. The Bottle Brush is a shrub that in spring-time is covered with clustering crimson spikes, shaped like the long rounded brushes used for cleaning bottles. The Waratah grows in New South Wales, Victoria and Tasmania. It is a stiff shrub, which sends up a tall woody stem, and this is crowned with a splendid cluster of flowers packed so closely that the cluster looks like one flower measuring perhaps six inches across. When grown in gardens, waratah shrubs have been known to carry more than five hundred of these great and splendid clusters. Because the waratah is such a very queenly flower and of such exceedingly rich colour it is often copied in stained-glass windows, and for other decorative purposes in colour; and because of its stately form it is copied also in stone and wood carvings for buildings and furniture.

But the loveliest flowers in Australia are of smaller growth. In the spring-time the multitudes of little dull-looking bushes become covered with beauty, while orchids breaking into tender colours help to make the Bush a fairy-land. There will be clumps and beds of boronia, and dillwynia, and epacris, and bossixe, and many kinds of these, besides dozens of other wild flowers in pink and white, cream, mauve, purple, yellow and other shades and colours.

Toward midsummer the white flannel-flower lifts its

beautiful shape in its chosen spots. Many people think that its quiet gentle beauty makes it the fairest of all Australian flowers. At Christmas-time two flowers appear which get their name from that happy holiday season. The Christmas Bush is covered with white flowers which seem to turn to red; but the red is really the fruit that has taken the place of the flower; only it looks more like flower than fruit, and is generally thought to be just the white flower turned to a rosier shade. It is used very much for Christmas decorations, and a sprig of it is generally stuck into the top of the Christmas pudding. The Christmas Bell is a rich yellow and crimson flower that comes around with the approach of Merry Christmas. But all the year round the Australian Bush will make some show of flowers for those who know where to look for them, unless dry hot winds at times have withered them.

It may be repeated that Australia is a great land with so many different climates in it from north to south, so that different parts of it have their own special flowers. Western Australia is very rich in wild flowers, and in the springtime acres of Everlasting Flowers, as they are generally called, may be seen in one patch, with others as large in all directions, and flowers of strange shapes and of many colours spring up elsewhere to carpet the country with their loveliness.

There are some growths that had better not be touched. The Nettle Tree is one of these. A touch of either its bark or leaves will give a most painful sting, which will spread over that part of the body and raise a swelling that may last for many days, and some of the pain may be felt for a week after.

This tree is not very common, and is very easily noticed. The Lawyer Vine is another thing to keep clear of. It is armed with sharp hooks turned backwards, and when once they get hold it is difficult to get free from them. But to make up for such an objectionable creeper, there are many lovely ones that festoon the trees and wreathe them with their flowers.

A very large and beautiful bunch of wild flowers from Australia was once sent to Queen Victoria. It was sent frozen in a block of ice, which was kept in the freezing chamber of the steamer on its way to England. When the ice was melted after its arrival, the great and good Queen could see the loveliness of these strange flowers which had grown in that part of her Empire farthest away. She had often read about them, but now she really saw and handled them; though only for a little while, as they soon drooped and withered after their long freezing.

CHAPTER XIX

THE BUSH: ITS ANIMALS AND BIRDS

THERE is one class of animals, called Marsupials, whose home is in Australia. A very few marsupials are found in other parts of the world, but in Australia they abound in great number and variety. The name Marsupial is taken from a Latin word meaning a pouch or bag, and is given to animals that grow a pouch in which to carry their young.

The largest of the marsupials is the Kangaroo. The giant kangaroo and the red kangaroo may grow to a length of six feet, not reckoning their tails. The kangaroo has very long hind legs upon which it can squat with its body erect, like a dog when it sits up begging. The fore legs are very short, and are not used at all when the kangaroo wants to get over the ground quickly. It does not run on four legs, but travels erect in great leaps, using its long thick tail as a sort of third hind leg to give it extra springing power. A kangaroo can take a long jump of from ten to twenty feet. It can take a high jump, too, clearing a fence up to eleven feet.

The kangaroo is a timid animal, and always moves off when it sees any one approaching. But it can be easily tamed; and may be taught to box very well, using its short fore legs, or paws. When it is chased and cannot escape it will get its back against a tree and fight fiercely, attempting to rip man or dog with the sharp claws of its powerful hind legs. Sometimes it will take refuge in a pool of water; and if a dog goes in after it, the kangaroo at bay will seize the dog, and hold it down under the water until it is drowned.

Australian marsupials are found in most various sizes, from the great red kangaroo down to a tiny pouched mouse. Some of the best known of the marsupials are the wallaby, the wallaroo, the native bear, the tree kangaroo, the opossum, the bandicoot, and the kangaroo rat.

The Native Bear, or more properly the Koala, is a curiously quiet, friendly animal, that will await one's coming without fear. It is a tree climber, and will sit apparently contented in a tree while it is shot at again and again, its thick close fur being sufficient armour against ordinary gun-shot. It can be tamed quite easily, and indeed is tame even its original wild state. Its friendliness becomes troublesome, for it likes to climb and sit on one's shoulder. It is about two feet long, and carries its young in its pouch until they grow too big for it, when it transfers them to its back until they are able to look after themselves.

The Wombat is another curious marsupial. It is something like a pig, and possesses sharp teeth and claws. It makes a burrow, and lives underground during daylight. If it is dug out it is sleepy and stupid in the light, but at night it goes abroad and is a quick and lively animal.

There are a great many kinds of Opossums. They make special use of their long tails. The ring-tailed opossum will curl its tail round the branch of a tree, and hang comfortably with its head downward. There is no fur on the lower part of its tail; and the skin is rough, preventing it from slipping when it is used to hang up by.

The strangest of all Australian animals is the Platypus, or Duck Mole, as it is sometimes called. It is twelve to eighteen inches long, with a short tail. What a mixture the platypus presents!—its body is covered with a beautiful, velvety fur; it has a bill like a duck; has no outside ears, but can hear sounds very quickly is web-footed for swimming, and has also claws for burrowing, lays eggs, feeds its young with its own milk; is an expert diver and swimmer and can also travel well on land. The platypus makes its home in the bank of a stream or lagoon, burrowing into the bank as far as twenty or even fifty feet. At the end of the burrow is a chamber in which its eggs are laid and hatched, and its young are reared. This animal with its strange combinations is a relic of far back ages. Somehow, when other animals disappeared or developed, it was left behind, and has never changed.

Another animal curiosity of Australia, a relation of the platypus, but not at all like it in appearance, is the Echidna, or Porcupine Anteater. It has a covering of quills, a very long narrow beak, and a long, sticky tongue. With its sticky tongue it is able easily to catch the ants on which it feeds. The echidna lays an egg, but does not hatch it in a nest. It puts the egg in its pouch, and carries it about until the young one is hatched. The young one lives there, feeding on its mother's milk until it is able to step out and begin life on its own account. The echidna burrows in the ground, digging in very quickly, so quickly that if an onlooker turns away for a minute or two it is out of sight. If an echidna is to be kept in confinement, it must be placed where the floor is of cement or something as hard, or it will dig its way out and escape.

The Dingo, or Native Australian Dog, called by the blacks of Queensland the Warrigal, is about the size of a small collie, and may have either silky or woolly hair. It is not a dangerous animal, except perhaps when very hungry; but it will do a great deal of damage among sheep; not content with catching and devouring what it needs, but killing a large number beside. The blacks are fond of tamed dingos, and will treat them quite as well as they treat their own children. Dingo pups are caught and tamed in blacks' camps; but in spite of the taming these dingos will often run off and take to their wild state again. The dingo howls, but does not bark. As soon, however, as it mixes with domestic dogs it learns to bark as they do.

The Flying Fox of Australia is badly named, for it is a bat, the largest of the bat family. Its body was supposed to resemble a fox; hence its name. It has a small body and huge wings which give it great strength and speed, measuring as they often do three feet from tip to tip. Flying foxes live together in immense numbers in lonely spots in the Bush. During the day they hang by their claws head downwards from the trees. At sunset they wake up and go abroad, sweeping off in flocks and flying long distances. They are fruit-eaters, spending their nights during fruit seasons in robbing orchards. They are not content to take what they need, but take a bite out of very large quantities, spoiling it for any household use. At times large shooting parties will go into the Bush where the flying foxes hang by hundreds and thousands, and will shoot them all day long. But when night comes there will still be black clouds of them flying off to orchards near and far. Owners of orchards often find it necessary to protect their trees with nets. Fortunately, these haunts of flying foxes are not very numerous, though troublesome enough.

There are no savage animals in Australia. In Tasmania, the Dasyure, often called the Tasmanian Devil, is a nasty fierce creature. In that Island there is also the Thylacine, or Tasmanian Wolf, which is active and fierce, doing much damage among sheep. But neither of these need be regarded as really dangerous savage animals. The animals of the Australian Bush are harmless, gentle creatures, and for the most part can be easily trained as household pets. It is a pity that the increase of settlement should drive so many of them from their ancient homes, and seriously reduce their number. The Governments are undertaking measures for the protection of some of them.

The birds of Australia are particularly beautiful and interesting. There are no more beautiful birds in the world than those of Australia. It has often been said that they have no song. That is quite a mistake; for though they do not warble and trill like English birds, very many of them have their own notes, which are exceedingly pleasant and musical.

The largest Australian bird is the Emu. It is a running and

not a flying bird. Its wings are very short, and the only use that can be made of them is as sails to help the bird in its running. An emu stands about six feet high, and is of a dull grey-brown colour. It has very long and powerful legs, with which it can kick backwards like a horse, and its kick is hard enough to break a man's bones. The emu lays from six or seven to as many as forty eggs in a season; the male bird helping to hatch the eggs. The nest is usually near some bushes, or under the shadow of a tree, but is little better than a hollow scratched in the ground with grass laid in and around it. Emu's eggs are good for food, and the flesh of an emu is said to have the flavour of beef. Oil is also obtained from it, and is used as a cure for rheumatism. The cry of the emu is a peculiar booming sound, varied at times with a sharp, shrill note.

These birds were found in great flocks in the early days of settlement. They are now found only in the remote back country. Occupation and fencing of the land have been bad for the emu. There is quite a possibility that the once numerous emu flocks will become extinct. It is a bird that needs a lot of room, and settlers, have regarded it as a nuisance, so that its destruction has been rapid. It is easily tamed, and will learn to stay around a house where it has been domesticated; but it is a bird of an uncertain temper, and may give any one an unexpected bite.

If the emu is the largest bird in Australia, the best known is the Laughing Jackass, or, to use the blacks' name for it, the Kookaburra. It belongs to the family of Kingfishers, and has a specially large and strong beak. It is a dull and clumsy-looking bird, but has a great deal of sense and courage, and certainly ought never to have been called a jackass. The great accomplishment of the kookaburra is snake killing. It will swoop down with all its force upon a snake, striking it and breaking its back with its powerful beak. This renders the snake helpless, and the kookaburra taking it in its beak proceeds to carry it up to a great height, from which it lets it fall to the ground. This action is repeated until the snake is dead. Afterwards, if the bird is hungry, it may swallow the snake, provided it is not too big for a meal. Sometimes, however, the attempt is made with a snake that is too large. Then having swallowed all it can, the kookaburra sits, a picture of unhappiness, with a long piece of snake hanging out of its mouth.

This bird has a jolly laugh, from which it gets part of its name. The laughing is generally done in company, three or four together working each other up into explosions of mirth. One will begin with a quiet "he-he-he," and then go on more loudly "ah-ah-ah." The others begin to see the fun, and chortle "he-he-he" also. By this time the first bird has reached a more explosive stage and is roaring out "oh-oh-oh." This is too funny for the others; and all join in a chorus of loud guffaws. Their laughter sounds so ridiculously real that it is hardly possible to listen to it without feeling inclined to join in the absurd chorus.

The Lyre Bird is remarkable for its beautiful tail-feathers, which stand up in the shape of a lyre, and for its marvellous power of imitating any and every sound. It has a rich full note of its own, but it mimics perfectly the notes of other birds, and also such sounds as the barking of a dog, the playing of a piano, the crying of a child, the noise of sawing wood—indeed, any sound it hears. One careful observer says that he noted twenty-five different imitations one after the other by a lyre-bird, including the "choo-choo" of a railway engine puffing up a steep incline some distance away. The lyre bird constructs not only a nest, but a sort of playing ground as well, in which it likes to show off its beauty.

The Bower Bird builds a most wonderful bower or playing ground, decorating it with any coloured things it can find and carry. The floor of this playing ground is covered by the birds with pebbles, shells, coloured seeds, bits of glass or metal, or anything bright. They will gather these by hundreds and arrange them according to their taste. When parading over them they will stoop to remove certain pieces, altering and improving the pattern. They gather flowers, too, and hang them upon the walls of the bower. This bird might well be called the Artist Bird. The blacks say that bower birds always go off to take a bath before entering their bower. This may or may not be so. It would be quite in keeping with their dainty taste that they should wash before proceeding to their Palace Beautiful.

There are in Australia mound-building birds; so called, because of the great heaps of earth and leaves and sticks they pile up for hatching their eggs. Some of these birds will bury their eggs several feet deep in such mounds, the heat of the rotting leaves serving to hatch them. A single heap may be large enough to provide for a number of birds; and one heap was found to measure 150 feet round.

The Native Companion is a bird found in large numbers in inland parts of Australia. It belongs to the family of Cranes, and is a tall bird about four feet high, on very long, thin legs. These birds will perform the most remarkable dances together. A flock of native companions may be seen to arrange themselves in a circle; then some will advance toward the centre, and after bowing to each other skip back to their places; now others come forward and do the same; next all jig round, and in and out as though in an arranged dance; the circle is formed again, and so the fun goes on with repeated bowings, hops and formal formations.

There are several Australian birds named after the call or cry they utter. One of these is the Whip Bird, or Coach-whip Bird. Its note is like the swish and crack of a whip. It really takes two birds, male and female, to make the complete sound: the male bird giving the crack, and the female the finishing touching. Another bird which has notes like the tinkle of a silver bell is called the Bell Bird. Another, an Owl, which cries dolefully through the night "mo-poke" or "more-pork," is called the Mo-poke. A pleasanter name is given to the Willy-wagtail, which twitters "sweet pretty creature," and so gets that as its name. Yet another is called the Razor Grinder, because of the whirring sound it makes. Yet more could be added to the list of names so given.

There are altogether in Australia 775 species of birds. The State of Queensland is particularly rich in bird-life, and 699 species are found there. Australian birds vary in size, from tiny little tits and finches and chats of many colours, looking almost like butterflies in the sun, up to great birds such as the eagle, the black swan, the bustard, cassowary and emu. There are more kinds of pigeons in Australia than in any other part of the world, some of them, such as the Bronze Wing and Crested Pigeon, being particularly handsome. There are sixty kinds of Honey Eaters, some having most beautiful plumage. So through long lists of delightful birds, vying with each other in plumage, it would be possible to continue to describe the abundant, happy bird life of the Bush.

To pass from beautiful birds to ugly snakes is a change indeed. But the life of the Bush is not all gentle marsupials and richly plumaged, sweet-voiced birds. Snakes, and other creeping things, come into it.

There are about 100 species of snakes—which sounds very dangerous. It is true also that about three-quarters of them are venomous. But only five common forms are really deadly. Fortunately, Australian snakes are very timid, and always get out of any one's way if possible. One may tramp through the Bush day after day and not see a single snake, though there may be a good many about. As soon as they hear a footstep, or the sound of the cracking of a dry stick underfoot, they glide away. Fortunately, too, the deadly snakes of Australia have short teeth, and if the bite is through even one thickness of clothing the poison is not likely to pass into the body of the person who has been bitten. It is wise, however, when walking through the Bush, just to look where one is treading, so as not to step on a snake that is too fast asleep to get out of the way. In the towns there are no snakes, and in all the most settled and populated parts of the country they are becoming fewer and fewer and are being gradually killed off.

The last word about the Bush must be of its fresh, sweet air and its golden sunshine. In Australia one may expect three hundred days of the year to be bright and sunny. When it rains it usually does so in good earnest, and gets it over and clears up quickly. Cricket might be played all the year through, but it is laid aside for a little while to give football a chance. The Bush is at its very best in the early morning. Then the air is so clear and light and fragrant that to breathe it is to have one's blood purified and one's brain cleansed. Then a gallop on horseback sets one hallooing for very lightness of heart, and the horse seems to enjoy it as much as the rider. Australia is the land of the open-air life. It is true the heat of summer is at times oppressive, but it is only for a short period of the year. In winter the tang in the air is in pleasant contrast to the warmth of the sun's rays. In parts the cold is more intense, and a fireside becomes a welcome spot. But always the year through with certain days excepted it is sunshine—sunshine. The call of the Bush is to picnic and play, with. the result that the Australians are the greatest holiday makers in the world.